SINGLE

Single Dads, book 1

RJ SCOTT

Love Lane Books

Copyright

Copyright ©2019 RJ Scott

Cover design by RJ Scott

Edited by Sue Laybourn

Published by Love Lane Books Ltd

ISBN 9781073072248

This literary work may not be reproduced or transmitted in any form or by any means, including electronic or photographic reproduction, in whole or in part, without express written permission. This book cannot be copied in any format, sold, or otherwise transferred from your computer to another through upload to a file sharing peer-to-peer program, for free or for a fee. Such action is illegal and in violation of Copyright Law.

All characters and events in this book are fictitious. Any resemblance to actual persons living or dead is strictly coincidental. All trademarks are the property of their respective owners.

Dedication

Always for my family

Also… For Laurie Peterson who wanted my first responder guys to take the kids from a group home on a camping/fishing trip.
Sorry, Laurie - you'll have to wait for book 2, but I promise this is exactly what Eric, Leo, and Sean will do.

Single

RJ SCOTT

ONE

Asher

Vin Diesel is outside my house.

It's two a.m., Mia is asleep, and I'm hallucinating that a Hollywood actor is outside my house in the San Diego suburbs.

"Open the door!" the big man bellowed, banging on the wood. I grabbed the nearest thing I could find to use as a weapon, then switched on the porch light that illuminated the area with the light of a hundred suns, and wrenched open the door. My attempt at acting like a hard-ass was undermined by the fact that my weapon was a citrus-yellow bowl my twin sister had made. It didn't help that I was wearing pajama bottoms that barely sat on my hips and a T-shirt emblazoned with a farting unicorn, but still I growled.

And there stood Vin Diesel himself.

Now that I was up close I could see it wasn't the *real* actor. Just someone who, in my state of exhaustion, appeared a hell of a lot like him. In my defense, my vision was blurry. This was my first night being completely and utterly alone with my brand-new baby daughter. No more sister backing me up, no more getting a few hours' sleep. Actually, I'd had no more than an hour's sleep at a time in the past three days. Too late to do anything about it, I wondered if this behemoth might have a weapon, because it was two a.m., he was swaying, and he was obviously off his head on something. Drugs. This had to be something to do with drugs.

Why didn't I pick up my cell phone first?

I'd forgotten my damn phone, and I'd only opened the door so the banging wouldn't wake Mia up, and I hadn't even considered this guy could be an armed intruder.

An armed intruder isn't likely to knock or shout so loud the whole neighborhood is probably peering out of their windows.

Also, I lived in a small house in a peaceful San Diego suburb, in a quiet cul-de-sac, where excitement was what happened last month when the guy at number six lost his garage remote.

Fake-Diesel stumbled back a little and winced up at the porch light, shielding his eyes and cursing.

"My keys," he mumbled and patted his pockets, pulling out a bunch of keys with a joyful whoop, then immediately dropping them on the ground.

"Who are you?" I stood right in the doorway and kept my voice low; anything not to wake Mia. I'd just gotten her to sleep, and if this Diesel wannabe woke her up with his asshole banging on my freaking door, then I would shove a dirty diaper in his face before calling the entire police department down on him. Or maybe a SWAT team consisting of parents who knew what it was to have a new baby who refused to sleep. An entire armed force of sleep-deprived adults would end up killing him.

Now, *that* would get him the fuck off my porch.

He straightened and blinked. Then he cruised me. Or at least it seemed as if he might have. Right here on my property, clearly stoned, he raked his gaze from my head to my toes and lingered in the middle for way too long.

"You're not them."

Oh, so he wasn't cruising me unless he identified his friends by staring at their crotches.

He swayed toward me, his eyes glassy, his hand outstretched.

"You have the wrong house," I shoved the hand away and stepped outside, before pulling the door half closed behind me.

The guy was big, way bigger than me but he was so unbalanced I thought I could take him down if he tried anything.

Fake-Diesel spaced out in an instant, and for a brief shining moment, I genuinely thought that he understood what I was saying. Then he began to cry, great rivers of silent tears running down his face.

"Jesus," I said, unsure what to do next. Should I comfort the complete stranger crying on my doorstep or call the cops or what?

"Sean!" the stranger yelled through the open part of the door. "Leo!"

What the fuck? You'll wake the baby.

"Shut up!" I snapped as loudly as I dared, and hoped to hell his shouting hadn't reached through the house and up to the very light sleeper that was my daughter.

"GUYS!" he yelled again, and this time, he pushed it too far. So I did what every sleep-deprived adult would do in my situation. I lost my cool and snapped.

Luckily, for him, the extent of my snapping was thrusting the fruit bowl toward him in the most threatening way I could imagine.

"You. Stop. Go. Away. Or I'm calling the cops."

He took a step back. Wide-eyed. "What? Who? Where's Sean? Is Leo home yet?"

"My name is Asher," I snapped.

"Why are you in our house?" The guy looked so confused. "Are you Sean's latest hookup? He likes pretty boys…" He stopped, blinking back tears. Should I be offended? At thirty-one, I was a long way past a boy or being called pretty, for fuck's sake. One more step back and my visitor would be tumbling down the steps from my wraparound porch. He fumbled in his pocket, pulled out an old flip phone, and stared at the screen before punching at buttons with his big fingers.

"Sean? Leo? Guys?" he pleaded and then took that one fatal step back, tumbling down the steps and into a chaparral broom so overgrown it gave him a soft landing. I toed off one of my fuzzy duck slippers, a gift from Siobhan last Christmas, and wedged my front door open before going toward the idiot. Before I reached him, he'd jumped up, swayed, and then was violently sick in the same bush he'd landed in. His cell was on the grass, still lit up, and a tinny voice was calling loudly for someone called Eric.

I assumed the guy decorating my chaparral broom was Eric, and I picked up the phone. "I don't know who the fuck *you* are or who *Eric* is, but I'm at 23 Birds View Court, La Jolla, and you need to get your ass over here now to get him before I call the damned police."

"Sorry? What was the address?" the man at the other end of the call asked.

What the hell?

"San Diego, La Jolla, 23 Birds View Court." He'd better not be living hundreds of miles away.

"I'll be there in… shit… will you look at that?"

I held the phone away from my ear, some kind of weird echo made it sound like the voice was coming from right behind me. Then, with a flurry of movement, someone walked past, scaring the shit out of me, and went straight to fake-Diesel-Eric.

"Eric?"

"I couldn't help any of them," the big guy said, and then, in my front yard, with puke down his shirt, he started to cry again. "We tried, but the doors…"

The man who'd appeared from the darkness gripped his shoulder. "Jesus. I'm sorry."

I still couldn't get a good look at the second man or understand why either of them was hugging it out in my yard, Eric deadly quiet, and the other man holding him upright.

"Sean, I couldn't do a thing…"

Evidently, the guy holding Eric up was the Sean who

he'd had been calling for, the one who seemed to live in my yard somewhere and liked pretty boys.

Maybe this is a dream? Maybe I'm still asleep. This is a whopping Alice in Wonderland *kind of nightmare.*

"Let's get you home, okay?" Sean said.

Eric pulled back, swayed a little, and Sean grabbed him. Then he turned to face me.

"Sean Roberts," he said and attempted to extend a hand to me but realized at the last moment he couldn't let go of Eric. "We moved next door last week."

"Go away." I'd had enough of people on my doorstep. So far, Mia hadn't woken up, and I might just get away with it. "Take your *friend* and go."

"We're sorry. Eric's not had a good night."

Mia's piercing cry split the night, and I closed my eyes and counted down from ten. "You morons have woken up my baby, for fuc—for goodness sake."

I left Sean and this Eric guy and slammed the door in their faces. No point in trying to stay quiet when Mia was awake. I stopped outside her room, calmed my temper, cooled my stress, and pasted a happy smile on my face. All the books said that with Mia only six weeks old, I was probably a blur to her, but I never wanted her to see me unhappy. If there was the smallest chance she understood complex layers of loneliness, fear, and anger, then I would keep working on pushing them behind a smile.

I placed the bowl on the edge of the hall table and headed straight for the crying. The scent in my room was that of the small, scrappy human who had taken over my life. It was a new baby smell, talc and cream, and warmth. I scooped her from her cot, feeling every tiny molecule of my stress vanish in an instant. Snuggled with her head up and under my chin, my hand supporting her tiny diapered rear, she mewled unhappily.

"Aww, Mia, I bet you're just as sad not to be sleeping as I am," I murmured to my sweet, precious baby girl. She couldn't have been hungry, or at least she shouldn't have been. She'd finished her last bottle a little while back, and I went through my emergency checklist, which was fuzzy and unfocused and lodged in the back of my mind somewhere under a desperate need to sleep. One thing the nurses had drummed into me, followed by my sister, was that routine was everything and I needed to learn all the checklists until they became second nature.

Second nature they weren't, not yet, but I could work through them step by step.

The room was warm, but not too warm, and Mia's crib was right up against my bed. She didn't feel hot to the touch, and with the sniff test carried out, I didn't need to change her diaper after I'd done so an hour earlier. Or thirty minutes. I couldn't quite recall the time. Only that it was dark and past midnight. Her crying lessened, and she wasn't hunting for a bottle like a baby bird. She lay against my chest, all soft and sweet and wanting her daddy to fix it all.

"It's okay, Mia. The shouting men have gone. I made sure of it."

She hiccupped, and I rubbed her back before picking up the embroidered pink blanket, a gift from our surrogate, and taking her out to the living room. We snuggled on the sofa, me and my girl, and she sprawled over my chest as I pulled the soft blanket over her. Within minutes she was slumbering again, and I fought napping myself long enough to get her back to her crib. My phone showed it was three a.m., Mia was asleep, and I climbed into my bed, scooting next to the open-sided crib, and for a little while I stared at the miracle that had changed my life forever.

Familiar fears rose inside me, the ones that had plagued me ever since I'd received the email about the successful implantation. Was I good enough? Was she okay? Why couldn't I have stopped a drunk man from shouting and waking her? She shouldn't know fear or anxiety. She should never be pulled from innocent sleep.

I was her dad, and she was my daughter, and I had never loved anyone or anything the same as I did Mia Francesca Haynes.

TWO

Sean

Eric and I made it back home, stumbling and with a lot of cursing from him. Our front door was no more than thirty feet away, and I'd left it wide open after answering the phone. Cap the black lab stood in the doorway, his tail wagging as he bounced with excitement, waiting for two of his favorite humans as they headed toward him.

"Move back, Cap," I instructed, and after a low woof, he danced aside and let me help Eric over the threshold. I closed the door, with Eric's weight leaning on me, and we were finally in. Cap sniffed around, sat back on his rump and held up a paw. God knows what he was trying to ask for.

"Let's get you in the shower," I murmured, but I wasn't sure Eric was capable of hearing everything. He was lost in a place that only another first responder could understand, in a frightening headspace filled with failure and death.

The last shift had been rough for the first responders

at a three-alarm fire. I worked in the Emergency Room, so it wasn't my job to be at the building. It wasn't *my* job to decide who to reach first as fire destroyed one of the upper floors. I hadn't been the one who'd watched people die just out of reach of safety. No, I was the lucky one out of all of this, because I'd made it all the way home before Eric called me. I'd never forget his words; I'd heard them before.

Shit. This is bad.

As soon as he'd hung up, not able to say anything else, I'd called the hospital where I worked, but Soledad Memorial didn't need me. The survivors of the fire were being taken to Mercy, and there was nothing I could do to help them or my best friend. When he'd called me a second time, hours later, drunk, his lieutenant speaking for him, saying he'd put him in a cab and send him home, I jumped out of bed and was ready to pick him up.

But the stubborn-ass firefighters who formed the rest of his shift were all, *he's strong; he'll be fine; we all will be; hey, let's have another drink; he's already left in a cab, so you can't pick him up.*

The three of us living in this house had wildly different ways of coping with the things we saw. When I felt as if I'd failed, I went for a run, then would come back and lock myself in the bathroom, taking a bath and thinking everything through. When it happened to Leo, who's a cop out of the eighth division, he questioned everything his faith ever taught him and took long lonely walks with Cap. But Eric? I understood why Eric was drunk because that was how *he* dealt with the tragedies, the pain, and the indescribable horror of not being able to save everyone.

I managed to do some general medical checks, then got his huge drunk ass in the shower. Keeping the water warm I washed his hair, scrubbed off the stink of vomit, and then wrapped him in one of the giant purple towels he loved. An extra-large one for the six-five behemoth that was firefighter Eric Lester. With Tylenol at his bedside, plus two bottles of water, I got him into his bed and even attempted to get underwear on him.

We'd been close since we were too young to remember, but that didn't mean I wanted to go rooting around his junk trying to get him into boxers. It was a losing battle because he wasn't exactly helping, so I gave up and just tucked the quilt around him. When I thought it was safe to leave, after I'd placed a trash can right by the bed, he tugged me to sit down next to him. He didn't sound as drunk now, but the emotions were raw.

"We tried, Sean. We couldn't get to the last floor. The people there were trapped, and the fire doors... they were locked... I tried."

I knew he did. I bet the entirety of Engine 63 did. I knew for sure that every single one of his shift would have put their own lives at risk to keep people safe.

"I know you did," I said firmly and squeezed his hand. "Try and get some sleep, and I'll be in my room if you need me."

"It wasn't safe," he blurted. "Fire doors... none of them..."

"I know," I said uselessly, just agreeing with everything he said.

"We need to hold someone acc—account—"

"Accountable," I finished for him.

"That," he muttered, then he closed his eyes, turning onto his side and curling into a fetal ball of misery.

I shoved his clothes into the wash, added my own, then padded in my shorts to my room, taking a shower to clean off the stink of puke, and more so to stand under the water and let the weight and heat of it work my shoulder muscles. Tragedies like the fire tonight, in a place a whole lot less fancy than this neighborhood, would be a call to arms. Politicians demanding change, condemning landlords. Then it would all fade away, the same as every other time. During my last shift, I'd removed three bullets from a ten-year-old caught in a drive-by shooting. Still, the guns were out there, and the noises the people in charge made were quieter each time.

I climbed into bed and rolled onto my left side, my drapes open to the night, and I could see the corner of our neighbor's house in the dim glow of the street lights.

We owed the man and his family a huge apology. Turning up at their house had been an honest, and very drunk, mistake from Eric. The three of us had only moved here at the end of last week, and even though we'd introduced ourselves to some of our neighbors, we hadn't met him or his family at all. Their house had been empty when we'd knocked. So tonight, maybe Eric gave the wrong address to the cab. Maybe he'd confused the houses, which stood next to each other and were mirror images of each other. All I know was that Eric throwing up in the big bushy bush thing wasn't a good way to meet the neighbors. I bet the poor guy in his pj's had gotten it in the neck from his partner after the baby woke up. Tomorrow, I'd go over with a bottle of wine or something to explain what had happened, or at least give the glossed-over summary of events.

This was only day five in our new house, and I'd been determined to make a concerted effort to become more sociable. The last place we lived had been a dive, and we were just as likely to get mugged by people living near us than make friends. This house was different; a nice area, the three of us sharing the costs of it, each owning a portion of it.

I fired off a quick check-in request to Leo, the other one of us living here, and put the cell back on the side table. We had this thing between us, to touch base, to let each other know we were good. Eric, firefighter, never had his damn phone on him, but he made the effort when he could. Leo, cop, was efficient and the one who'd initiated this circle jerk that was the three of us letting each other know where we were. Then me, an ER doctor, the one who had to defend the fact that he was arms deep in blood and guts as the reason he couldn't get to his phone. I think Leo despaired of us; actually I *know* he did. My cell vibrated, and I pulled it out.

Long night, coffee shit, on my way home.

I wasn't going to sleep knowing Leo might want someone to talk to, so I got up and made fresh coffee; the three of us had shifts that were all over the place, and sometimes the only thing that kept us going was caffeine. When Leo arrived home, he cast a worried look toward Eric's room. I subtly shook my head and handed him a mug of coffee. He fell on it like a starving lion on fresh meat and then scrubbed at his eyes, fussing over Cap, who jumped around him and then leaped up next to him on the sofa and curled into his dad, his nose on Leo's knee and his tail wagging gently against the leather. Leo buried his hand into Cap's fur, and his voice broke.

"A family of five," he said and closed his eyes. "Mom, dad, three kids—they were trapped on the seventh floor. Smoke had already killed them before the fire got there. No fire doors on the floors below, it was like a chimney."

We took a moment to consider the horror of that loss, and Leo made the sign of the cross on his chest. He was a good Catholic boy, from a huge Italian family, most of whom were cops, and even though he'd long since lapsed, I'd seen him pray silently after a bad day. Hell, after any day.

"Eric got drunk," I said and poured my own coffee. I was on shift at ten, and it was already three in the morning. I couldn't see me getting much sleep, not when Eric might need me.

"I don't blame him. He was on floor clearance, tried to get through the door. I don't even want to think about what he heard…"

"I guessing you were called in as well?"

"After the fact."

That was all he needed to say. He'd probably been part of the team who'd taken witness statements, worked the scene. We sat in silent contemplation for a few minutes, lost in our own thoughts, and then I couldn't avoid telling him what had happened when Eric came home.

"He knocked on the wrong door, woke up a baby, pissed off our neighbor."

"Ouch." Leo winced.

"The guy said he was going to call the cops, but I got Eric away. We owe him an apology, or at least Eric does. We haven't been in this neighborhood a week, and our shit is already spilling over."

"It's a one-off. They'll understand when you tell them."

"Or not." The three of us didn't go around telling people about the crap in our lives. They didn't want to hear all the gory details that messed with our heads on occasion. I exchanged a pointed look with Leo, who simply nodded because he understood. "I'll take them over some wine."

Leo frowned and glanced around him at the piles of boxes in our front room; not one of us had managed to unpack a single thing. "Do we even have wine?"

"We will after I buy some." I wobbled as I stood, exhaustion making me slow. I had managed to get some sleep before I knew Eric was on his way home drunk, but it hadn't been enough. Then there was the guy on the porch all hissing and spitting, in pajamas, fuzzy duck slippers, bare-chested. He was all kinds of sexy, and I could think that privately, despite him being off-limits to a bunch of idiots like us, given he had a family and we hadn't even officially met. I checked in on Eric on my way back, and he was on his side, sleeping. He'd be in there processing everything in his dreams, or at least I hoped so. By tomorrow, he would have compartmentalized it all.

And whether that is a good or bad thing, it was what we did.

THREE

Asher

Mia woke at five, and I was instantly awake at the slightest sound. Her eyes were open, and she stared at the ceiling, waving her hands and curling her legs. She'd been active in the womb. At least that is what my surrogate had said, and I had no reason to disbelieve her. At one of the scans I'd attended, the pediatrician had shown me Mia's heart, her tiny fingers, and pointed out she was hiccupping as she moved. She'd been less than real at that moment; just a promise of something that was going to change my life forever.

Something I could plan for. The best crib, the most ergonomic stroller, a beautifully decorated nursery, formula, emergency numbers, and twenty-four new baby books. Not to mention sleepers in all different colors, hats, tiny coats… the list was endless, but I'd been equipped to the hundredth degree. Not that I knew what half of the things I'd bought were for, and I doubted I'd need most of it.

I'd like to have said I was prepared, but nothing could have prepared me for the day Mia had been handed to me. Not even the tons of books I'd waded through. Some of them explained that I should sleep when the baby did. But what happened when I was so busy watching to see if my baby was still breathing that I couldn't sleep at all?

The books said nothing about the terror that gripped me when I was the only one who could help this precious child who owned my heart.

"Morning, Mia," I murmured and managed to use the bathroom and get back before the snuffles and soft movements gave way to something more insistent. I skirted pieces of the now broken yellow bowl which I clearly hadn't pushed far enough back. Somehow I made it to the kitchen without shredding my feet, and added the clear up to my list. Then I measured everything perfectly, made up a bottle, and ignored the call of coffee. Maybe one day I'd be organized enough to have both, but right now, Mia was the priority. I took her to the garden-room that faced my back yard, and we sat on the small sofa there. She took her whole bottle, her hands opening and closing as she sucked, and then she was done. The spit-up on my navy sleep T-shirt was expected, and yet again I regretted forgetting the cloth by the bottles.

One day I'd get this right. One day I'd be the perfect dad.

Right now, I missed my twin Siobhan and her boisterous family. Mia and I had stayed in her garage conversion after collecting Mia from the hospital, and for just short of six weeks, I'd had Siobhan to turn to if I needed help. Now it was time for me to start a life on my own or at least a life where it was me and Mia alone. Rain beat on the glass roof, a soothing, hypnotizing noise, and I cradled my little girl in the garden room, lulled by the sound of it.

"I wished for you," I began and slid down in the seat as she cuddled into me. "When the wish came true, it created a perfect tiny miracle." She moved a little and caught my thumb in her fist, holding it tight. Just six weeks old and she knew that she could hold on to me. Before her, I truly felt my heart had been empty, but now we were a family. "You and I against the world, Mia." *I love you so much my heart hurts.*

I wanted to sleep, but I couldn't; too hyped up from being woken. I should clear up the bowl, but my back ached, my legs ached, in fact, everything ached. So I opened my laptop one-handed and caught up on a couple of emails as I yawned.

How many other new parents are out there, unable to sleep and utterly alone? More specifically, how many single dads.

Did they all feel so totally overwhelmed? I closed down my email and opened a browser, dimming the brightness on the laptop when my eyes began to burn. Then I typed *single new daddy help lonely* into Google and pressed search.

There were one hundred and thirty-nine million hits

or more. I couldn't read how many zeroes there were with blurry eyes. There was a lot of daddy porn to wade through, then pages dealing with bereavement and separation, and a useful link to the top ten apps I should have on my iPhone if I was to become a successful parent.

Talk about pressure. I wonder if the apps give you points for everything you do right.

I bookmarked the app for later, went back up to the search parameters, and added the word *gay*, *glbtq*, and *surrogate*, in the hope they would bring up a whole new set of more appropriate results. There were a couple of forums, but the one that caught my eyes had a rainbow logo and the letters *SDT*, which stood for Single Dads Together. I scrolled through some of the open posts, which were few and far between. This was a private forum I needed to sign into to get deeper, but on the surface, I wasn't sure it was my kind of place. One featured open post was by a dad of three called Nick, who'd lost his husband, another had a man talking about overseas adoption. They appeared to be the two guys who ran the forum, and at first glance, I wasn't able to see if there was someone on there like me.

Neither of them had made the decision to start a family on their own, and I felt unaccountably alone. Maybe no other man thought that they could be an effective lone parent to a baby girl? Guilt twisted in my chest, abruptly turning to anger. I wasn't supposed to be on my own. Darius was meant to be here as well.

Or at least he'd been present at the concept and ideas stage, and he'd interviewed surrogates. Even if he had sat on his phone for most of them, saying I was the better person to choose. After all, he'd convinced me that it should be my sperm, which helped to create our child, so I should be the one to select the surrogate. I should have known then, but I wasn't going to wallow in all of this shit now. Determined, I joined the forum, and in the bit where it asked me who I was and why I wanted to be on there, I spoke from the heart.

My name is Asher Haynes, and I'm gay. I have a daughter, who is six weeks old, through surrogacy. I just left my sister's house, and I'm home now. I chose to have Mia alone. I am alone.

I closed my laptop, and when Mia stirred, I changed and fed her. With her dozing on my chest, we sat together in the garden room for a while longer, and somehow I managed to quell the panic fluttering in my chest.

Siobhan said I would be fine, that I was going to be a wonderful dad, and that I was a great uncle. With the freaky twin connection we had she sometimes knew me better than I knew myself. Only, uncles can hand their nieces and nephews back. I couldn't do that. I didn't *want* to do that. When it was obvious I wasn't going to shut my brain down and my stomach growled with hunger, I decided to head to the kitchen for cereal. The first thing I spotted was the remains of the bowl from last night. Unluckily, the bowl had been the victim of my exhausted clumsiness, and tiny pieces of ceramic were scattered everywhere.

I bent to pick up a shard one-handed, although why I did that, I don't know, dropping it when it sliced into my hand. I didn't care because I didn't have any energy left *to* care. I picked my way through the fragments again, and back to the garden room. I'd really have to make the effort to clean it up later. The wound bled, but I wrapped it in a towel, and it wasn't as if it hurt. Then I think I maybe slept an hour. A sleep made up of fitful ten-minute naps interspersed with waking up in a cold sweat, a panic gripping me that Mia wasn't breathing, that somehow I'd lost the only important thing to me in my entire messed-up life.

Every time I checked her, she was fine, and I ignored the blood from my cut staining the towel there. With a sense of peace, I held my baby girl and changed her, then gave her a bottle when she woke up. She slept in my arms under the glass roof, and it was when I felt myself drift off that I decided I needed to get back to bed. Only, the hall was obviously still littered with pottery, and everything that had happened in the dead of night became real. With Mia in one arm, I refused to think about Sean or Eric or my chaparral broom or the smashed bowl. I'd sweep it all up later, hire a gardener to fix the bush, maybe clean the kitchen, find some coffee, and get a shower.

A shower sounded so damn good.

I stroked Mia's soft hair as I settled her in her crib and was immediately lost in thought. Everything I'd ever had or wanted was wrapped up in my daughter.

"I hope you'll love me," I said and swallowed the emotion in my throat. "I'll try and be a good man for you. I'll be the best daddy."

The person I became would be wise and focused, and

I would learn to love tea parties with teddies and dolls. I would patch up scraped knees, teach Mia all the things I'd learned so far in my life—for what they were worth. I'd show her when it was right to keep secrets and help her recognize when she should share, and most of all, I would help her find out what she wanted to be in this world. She would never make the same mistakes as me. I wouldn't allow anything to hurt her. She was my world now, and I would protect her and love her with every fiber of my being. She would be safe.

I would make sure of it.

FOUR

Sean

The wine I bought for Mr. Fuzzy-Slippers in the morning as part of my apology wasn't expensive, but it wasn't for lack of money, just choice. The small gas station carried the cheaper lines, but they did have flowers for Mrs. Fuzzy-Slippers and a brightly colored magazine with a teddy bear on the front. I didn't know how old the baby was, but I thought I had all my bases covered unless there were older children in the house as well. I didn't recall any of the neighbors we met talking about the family next door, although we hadn't stopped and talked to a lot of them, as moving, then shifts had swallowed our free time.

"Let's do this."

I tugged my shirt straight, ran a hand through my hair, which needed cutting about as urgently as my closet needed updating. No one saw my street clothes when I wore scrubs, so who cared whether my shirt was ironed or my jeans clean. The last thing I wanted was to come across as something less than the experienced doctor that

I was. After last night, we'd have been lucky to see respect from our neighbors, let alone become friends. I took the steps up to the porch and thanked the heavens it had rained and cleaned up whatever dinner Eric had left in the bush.

Checking the time once more, and assuming there were children here meant the entire family would be up, I knocked on the door and waited. I had three sisters, and all of them had children, and sleeping in was nonexistent to the point they told me they'd forgotten what they were.

I heard some banging inside, a few curses, and the door opened in a hugely dramatic fashion. Fuzzy-Slippers-guy stared at me, and he was exhausted.

"What?" he asked.

I thrust the wine at him, "For you," I said, then waggled it when he didn't take it. Then I remembered the flowers and magazine. "For your family." He stared at me, then the apology gifts I'd brought with me. "We just wanted to say sorry, Eric, Leo, and me. It won't happen again."

Of course I was lying. Who knew if it would happen again? None of us could control the kind of things we dealt with, and sometimes it was all too much. As it had been for Eric.

Just sometimes.

Call it a well-trained eye or seeing the way he swayed, but something wasn't right. Which was when I saw the blood.

"You're bleeding," I said and stepped closer.

He blinked at me, then looked down at his hand.

"Yeah, I cut myself," he managed, staring at it as if he had X-ray vision that was going to securely fix what appeared to be one hell of a deep cut. He opened and closed his fist, and blood oozed out as he opened the cut.

"Do you want me to take a look at it?" I asked and watched him think that one through. "I'm a doctor," I added, trying to be as helpful as I could to his decision-making process.

"I'm fine." He wiped his hand down his chest, leaving a smear of scarlet. Quite clearly he wasn't fine at all. I cracked my neck and stepped up to his doorway, peering behind him and assessing the situation. Shards of pottery littered the floor inside, and there was blood, but I wasn't sensing murder and mayhem, more misfortune and tiredness. I pressed his arm, guiding him to step back to the right and away from the majority of the shards, and he didn't stop me as I moved him into the kitchen, which was a mirror layout of ours. I sat him on the nearest stool and then considered the wound. Blood had dried around the cut, which extended from the fleshy part of his hand to the base of his little finger.

"Wait here," I said, crossing the field of sharp pottery before opening the door. I couldn't see a key to lock it, and this *was* an emergency, so I left it open as I jogged back to our house. I thundered up the stairs to my room and grabbed the house medical kit. I had responsibility for anything medical in the house, Eric was in charge of fire safety, but up to then we hadn't worked out what Leo was in charge of, even though he said he was on-site security. When I passed through the front room, I caught sight of Leo sprawled half on and half off the sofa, an empty beer bottle clutched to his chest. So much for security; if I'd been in less of a hurry, I'd have found a Sharpie and drawn on his face.

Heading back next door, I let myself back in. The guy hadn't moved.

"I don't know if you remember, but my name is Sean?" He watched me blankly. "I'm an emergency room doctor at Soledad Memorial, and I just moved in next door." Still nothing. If I hadn't seen this before, I'd wonder if he was catatonic, but the red eyes, the stubble, the hair sticking up on end, and the baby spit-up smell on his pajama bottoms, led me to an educated guess that this was classic new-baby syndrome. "What is your name?"

"What?"

"Can you tell me your name?" I used my firmest doctor tone.

"Asher Haynes, Ash."

"Okay, Ash, first I need to check the wound for debris." I talked to him the whole time I worked on the injury as I closed the wider part of the wound with tiny butterfly bandage and wrapped the hand in a light bandage. I did consider explaining how he should see his family doctor for follow-up, but thought I'd leave that for later; maybe write it down somewhere for him or his partner or whoever.

"What the hell was your friend Derek thinking, getting drunk and making all that noise?" Ash blurted.

"You mean Eric."

"Whatever."

"This morning I'm sure he has the hangover from hell, but he'll be okay."

Ash frowned. "No, I mean, you're a doctor. Shouldn't you explain to your *friend* about the excesses of alcohol and what it can do to him."

He was so damn serious, but I balked at explaining why Eric had gotten so blind drunk. It wasn't my story to tell.

"He had his reasons." At least Ash took the hint and didn't ask any more questions. "Is your wife or partner here?"

"No."

"Maybe you should call them?" I prompted.

"It's just me, on my own. I'm a daddy on my own." His tone grew belligerent, as if he was daring me to say something about it all.

"Okay," I said. I'd seen all kinds of families in the ER from moms and babies with a crowd around them to a single mom entirely on her own with her baby. Sometimes, if the mom couldn't be saved, it was a baby on their own.

Maybe this is what had happened to Ash? Had he lost his partner?

The sound of wailing filled the house, a baby waking and needing attention. The instant the noise reached the kitchen, Ash was up and off his chair, stumbling, righting himself, taking a baby bottle, and grabbing a carton of ready prepared formula from a huge pile of similar cartons, before taking the stairs as if the hounds of Hell were on his heels. How he managed to move that fast I don't know, but I watched him leave, safe in the knowledge that he wasn't in immediate danger from bleeding out.

I was about to go, but I couldn't in all conscience do that with deadly shards all over the floor. So I swept up the pottery, considered leaving the bits in case he wanted the bright yellow parts to be put back together, then decided that whatever it had been was never going to be fixed. However, I didn't want to dump it all into the garbage, so I tipped it all into an empty ice-cream container from the recycling bin. With that done, I had no reason to stay, but something made me go back into the kitchen. People didn't leave their neighbors in a mess like this if they could help. Humming along with Pink playing softly on my phone, I rinsed plates, loaded the dishwasher and set it going, then washed and sterilized all the bottles that had been piled on one side.

The sterilizer was exactly the same as the one that my oldest sister Rosie had, and with the bottles in a neat row on the side, I made fresh coffee for when Ash came down. He had one hell of a lot of those instant baby-milk cartons, the kind people used in emergencies, but there were also tubs of formula, and at first count, twenty-four brand new, still in their wrappers, pacifiers.

After five minutes, the crying had stopped, but since then, everything had been super quiet. I guessed the baby was being fed. I let myself out, the scent of coffee filling the hallway, and debated leaving the house at all because I couldn't lock the front door. Finally, I came up with a solution: I would keep an eye on it from our house. Then I jogged home and sought out Leo, who was up and doing yoga in the fourth bedroom that we'd dedicated to fitness. At the moment it held a yoga mat and some weights, but one day there might even be a treadmill in there. Who knew?

I didn't sit down, because I could only see Ash's front door if I stood. Cap was in his typical I'm-a-dog position as close to Leo as he could get, and I waited until Leo was aware I was there. That gave me time to think about Ash, with his dark soulful eyes. He was trying very hard to be the most awesome dad ever, and one day he'd get past the exhausted stage. He'd probably read all that he needed to, had all kinds of procedures in place, but hadn't figured out the mess that was real life. It was kind of endearing in a sexy kind of way.

Asking him out for a drink was a thought I had as I'd bandaged his hand. From a purely physical point of view, I was attracted to tall, dark, and moody guys, but I'd never dated a new dad before or anyone with children. He'd said he was alone, but that didn't mean he played for my team or would even be interested. Still, I couldn't stop the X-rated thoughts that popped into my head.

Leo finished his breathing exercises and stretched his muscles before sitting on the mat cross-legged.

"That was one hell of a long sorry to our neighbor."

"Huh?"

"Your note on the chalkboard said you were apologizing, and that was two hours ago."

"Oh, yeah, well, Ash is all alone over there, and he'd hurt himself. I had to help him. Then I tidied his place up a bit."

"*Ash* hurt himself?" His tone was teasing, and then

abruptly, he corrected himself. "Wait, hurt himself how?" This time his voice held a war of reactions that a cop like him would feel. The "hurt himself accidentally or deliberately," question unspoken.

"Cut his hand on pottery, so I patched him up." No need to tell Leo that I'd then made coffee while I cleaned up the aforementioned pottery and put the kitchen back to rights. Not to mention how I'd handled sterilizing bottles. There was only so much a person shared with one of their best friends before they got the piss ripped out of them at every available moment.

"Okay then, as long as it was just that." He wiped his sweaty face with a towel and looked at me expectantly. "And?"

"And what?"

"You have never willingly set foot in this room, but now you won't move? You clearly have things to say."

I huffed and then waited a little while. "You know I like running for real and yoga bores me."

"One day I'll get you to sit still long enough to center yourself."

I ran a hand from my throat to my belly. "I'm perfectly centered, thank you very much."

"So you say."

"Whatever," I began. "Leo, I need to ask you something?"

I think maybe I sounded way too serious because Leo stood up, then leaned on the window sill next to me. "Is it Eric? Is he okay?"

"I haven't seen him yet." He wasn't on duty for another forty-eight hours, he was *presumably* hungover, and he was *probably* staying in his room debating whether to even get out of bed. "It's not Eric, although I'm going to cook him some food before I go on shift. Can you make sure he eats something?"

"Of course," Leo said. "So, in all seriousness, if it isn't Eric that's worrying you, what's so important that you're messing with my Zen?"

"The guy next door..." I pressed my fingers to my temples, not quite knowing what to say about Ash.

"Number twenty-three, Asher Haynes, unmarried, no dependents that I could find, but maybe that has changed since the check if there's a baby now. No criminal history, degree in game design from MIT, works from home, pays his taxes, owns a red Hyundai Tucson."

"Wait? You checked him out?"

"I check everyone out," Leo dismissed, then looked at me. "Is it just him you're worrying about, or do you want to know about the speeding ticket that Jeremy Graves at number 15 received two years back or the fact that Gina Lazar at 10 was a stripper and got pulled on four separate occasions for solicitation?"

"Gina? Isn't that the woman who brought that tuna casserole on our first day and came on to Eric?"

"One and the same."

Gina Lazar was a big-chested, loud, funny woman in her late fifties, who hadn't seemed that worried when Eric explained he was gay. She'd just asked if he had any straight friends, and I'd never seen Eric go so scarlet.

"I genuinely don't want to know that about Gina."

"But you're worried about the guy next door?"

"He's a new dad, looked like shit, but he'd cut himself, and there was blood and a smashed bowl, and he seemed kind of out of it."

"Maybe he needs you to go over again and kiss his boo-boos." Leo was teasing me, I knew that, and I shoved his shoulder.

"Whatever, freak."

I left the mobile security camera at a side window, videoing anyone who approached Ash's house, and had the monitor propped up on the work surface. Then, with it in place, I stood in the kitchen, rinsing mugs and filling the dishwasher. There was something very therapeutic about tidying up and looking at a clean kitchen. I could see the backyard of the next house, but there was no sign of Asher Haynes or his baby. I shouldn't worry. I mean, if our resident cop wasn't concerned, then I had to think it was all okay. Only, Leo hadn't seen Ash or watched him vanish to see to a crying baby, not caring about the fact that a total stranger was in his house as he stumbled up the stairs.

"Maybe I should go over later," I said to no one in particular.

"What?" Eric asked from behind me.

I turned as he opened the fridge and pulled out a carton of orange juice. I steeled myself to be the best friend, the one who understood him, but he appeared calm. During my psych rotation, I'd learned all about bottling things up, but how could I even ask Eric to confront what he'd seen and talk to me? I wouldn't talk to him about the things I'd seen.

He actually seemed okay, tired, a little red-eyed, and

he had a wicked bruise on his temple, but his breathing sounded good, and from a medical point of view, he wasn't in need of urgent help. That was all I could do for him right now, and I knew that.

Eric shook the carton, then drank straight from it, finishing what was left and tossing the empty container into the recycling.

"You okay?" I asked.

"No," he said with absolute certainty and hip-checked me out of the way of the coffee pot. "But I will be."

FIVE

Asher

San Diego sunshine poured through the blinds, and a strip of light hit my face. For a moment I stretched like a cat, all my muscles deliciously loose. In that millisecond, I was just Asher Haynes, single dude with no responsibilities, and then in the next breath, awareness of who and what I was hit me hard. And it was beautiful.

I rolled to my side and stared right at Mia.

She's not breathing. She's still.

Then I saw the rise and fall of her chest, and right there was the miracle that was my beautiful daughter, so close I could reach out and touch the wispy hair on her head.

So close I could smell she needed her diaper changed.

But she was still sleeping, and I was taking the chance to grab a pee, and even managed the quickest shower on record, which was more of a walk-in-the-water dash.

I managed both of these things in the space of a couple of minutes, and by the time I walked naked into my bedroom, Mia had begun to stir, a soft murmuring as her instinct for food and a clean diaper hit her. There was the scent of coffee in my room.

Why was there the scent of coffee in my room?

"Hey, little brother!"

I yelped, covered my groin, and tripped over a pair of discarded running shoes, all in the time it took my idiot sister to snort with laughter.

"What the hell, Shiv?" I snapped and turned my back to my twin, grabbing the nearest clean underwear and covering my junk.

"Nice ass," she said and snorted again. "Your face when I said hello was comic gold. I wish I'd been filming it because, dude, you're so funny."

"Siobhan, I've had two hours sleep, and I will kill you."

She smiled at me but then grew serious. "What the hell?" she asked and took my hand, peering down at the soaking wet bandage. I'd forgotten about that, and it had collected water and was dripping on my carpet. "You've only been home twenty-four hours."

"Shit," I muttered and stared down at it, attempting to pull memories from my hazy mind. "I cut my hand, but it's okay. A doctor…"

She wasn't listening. She dropped my hand and then scooped Mia out of her crib. She did the sniff test, the one I'd seen other new parents do to their baby's diapers. It was the one I promised myself I would *never* do until I realized it was the only way to tell if something lurked inside. I knew her diaper needed changing, but if I admitted that I'd left her sleeping to grab a shower, would that make me a bad dad in my sister's eyes?

Even though she was cool with it now, Siobhan's first reaction to my plans had been horror. Not that she thought it was wrong, but she'd immediately suggested that it made sense for her to be the one to carry her niece or nephew instead of a surrogate. Given she was the mom of two and had nearly died giving birth to my niece, there had been no way I was ever going to agree to her suggestion. That was when the shit hit the fan. She hadn't spoken to me over that heated debate for two weeks and three days. I knew it was that long because she was my twin, and we talked or texted every day, and those seventeen days of being alone had been horrifying.

Thankfully, she'd finally accepted my decision, backed up by some interference run by her husband, Dan, who was on my side. Then, with Dan overseas, she'd suggested I stay with her after picking up Mia, just to learn and have someone close.

I'd only done it because she promised our mom wouldn't be involved.

Mom-issues, I have them.

Siobhan changed the diaper, using all the tricks she had taught me, wrapped the stinky one up and tied the scented sack. Then she lifted Mia and cradled her.

"Hello, my sweet precious Mia," she murmured, and in that moment, with the sun shining and casting a halo around the two most important women in my life, I forgave the fact that she'd let herself into the house and then scared the shit out of me.

Talking of which, if Siobhan was there, I could go back in and get a real shower, maybe even shave? Maybe I telegraphed that to her because she patted my chest. "Shave, shower for longer than ten seconds. I'll make us lunch and see you downstairs in thirty."

There were two people I trusted with Mia. Me being one of them, I had every faith in Siobhan. But as she walked away, I stood there with my arm outstretched in fear, like some guy in an old painting whose kid was being taken away forever. I was bereft, scared, tired, my hand hurt, and all I wanted was for Mia to come back.

Siobhan turned as I knew she would—it was that freaky twin connection we had going on, and she could feel my fears. "I have her," she murmured gently.

"Be careful walking down the stairs," I said because that was all I could think of saying.

She could have done her normal twin thing, made some sarcastic comment about how she'd been using the stairs for all of her thirty-one years, but she didn't. She smiled in reassurance.

"It's okay, little brother."

And just like that, it was.

Sue me if I watched them go downstairs, and only moved when they were at the bottom. She knew I was watching, and gave me the finger. I couldn't blame her for that.

Back in the bathroom, I stripped off the outer bandage and then didn't know what to do next as I examined the neat row of tiny butterfly bandages. Had the doctor-guy said I shouldn't get it wet? Jeez, I didn't actually remember much of what he'd said. I didn't even recall his name. Hell, I had a hard time recalling my own. In fact, my entire impression of him was that he was my neighbor and he lived with an alcoholic friend, or at least a friend who got so blind drunk he couldn't even find his way home.

Also, that he'd brought wine and flowers, and a comic or something like that.

Oh, and he had blue eyes and soft blond hair. I wasn't dead, and I certainly wasn't blind.

I shaved as best I could despite the fact that every movement made my hand hurt like a bastard. I had to wet shave because I'd gone past sexy stubble and driven right on through to ragged, homeless-guy semi-beard.

I spied a plastic grocery bag stuffed with baby wipes of which I had a year's worth. They had been a last-minute desperate purchase only a day before Mia was born, the kind of thing I felt I had to have in the house to become the perfect dad. It turned out all I needed to do was be there when she needed me, and that it wasn't about the wipes, pacifiers, or the heap of cute shape toys I'd bought and stored in her colorful nursery. With some fumbling and a small helping of ingenuity, I tipped out the contents and tied the bag around my hand and then turned on the water. It was hot, the shampoo frothed up, the water felt different on my smoothly shaven face, and I spent a good deal of time soaping everything. Normally, this alone time was the perfect time to pull out my favorite fantasy and enjoy the solitude.

Only I didn't like that I was up here and Mia was downstairs, even if she was with my sister.

Part of me hoped that one day I wouldn't suffer

separation anxiety, even when I went to use the bathroom. The remainder of me, the part that was besotted with Mia, was telling my sensible side that Mia was my life now. The life I wanted and that I loved.

I dressed in clean jeans and the softest T-shirt I could find—Mia adored snuggling into soft material—and headed downstairs. I heard Siobhan murmuring to Mia and followed that and the scent of more coffee to the kitchen.

The immaculately tidy kitchen.

Not one single sign of the cereal I'd spilled, or the plates I'd left, or the bottles that had needed cleaning and sterilizing.

"Thank you," I said with so much gratitude I came off as sarcastic.

"I've held babies before," Siobhan deadpanned.

I took Mia from her and held her close. "And you managed to clean the kitchen at the same time? I swear I'm still at the point where I can barely remember to breathe, let alone multitask."

She raised a perfectly shaped brow. "This wasn't me, Ash. Are you forgetting what you've done?"

"No. I didn't…"

She crossed her arms over her chest. "Also, Ash, your front door was unlocked."

"Shi— Oh." Stopping myself from cursing was hard enough when I was awake, but tired, the words were slipping out.

"I just walked in." Then she smirked at me. "But not before I got jumped by the hottie from next door."

"Huh? Who? What? What do you mean a hottie

jumped you? Do we need to call the cops?" I was spiraling into panic.

She placed a hand on my chest, her usual message that I needed to stop and listen to her. "I parked, and this gorgeous blond sprinted out of the next house, vaulted the perimeter fence in one bound, and honestly, I'm a married woman, but that was a hundred kinds of sexy."

"Huh?" I repeated.

She shook her head. "Sean *something*. Tall, blond, striking bright blue eyes, all kinds of badass as he stalked over."

That sounded like the caring doctor guy, but I hadn't recalled his name. I might have forgotten that, but I wasn't going to forget he was sex on legs. I was tired, not blind.

"Why did he jump you? What do you mean?"

"He said he had to leave you in the house with an unlocked front door, so he's been monitoring anyone who arrived, which turns out it's just me. He was very charming, but he asked me why I was here. So I told him I was your evil twin and I was coming to steal the innocent baby to take her back to the cult."

I massaged my temples to release the pressure building there. "Siobhan, what the hell—"

"I'm joking. I explained I was your sister, that I was the better twin, and how you were a complete idiot and a new dad, and I was coming to check on you because you only left my house two days ago, but I had a twin-feeling that you were struggling."

I groaned. I couldn't help it; Siobhan had this way about her that was all sass and confidence, and now my next-door neighbor, my *hot* next-door neighbor, probably thought I was an idiot.

He already knows that from last night and this morning.

"Why did you tell him I was struggling?"

She stared at me as if I was talking an alien language. "Ash, you have a new baby, you're managing this on your own, it's new to you, and you're running on limited sleep. Of course you're struggling, so I just wanted to check in on you. Don't you remember when Evan was born, and Dan was overseas, and I was doing everything on my own? There's no shame in admitting you need help."

I tried to think of something clever to say, but she had a point. Dan was in the military and had been deployed for both of his babies' births, and Siobhan had done everything alone, including nearly dying giving birth to Debs, her youngest.

"Also, interesting fact," she said as she made a bottle and closed the nearest cupboard doors with her feet, all at the same time. One day I, too, may be able to multitask with that much agility. "The hottie is gay."

I didn't put that statement in context, too envious of her ability to juggle all the things I struggled with at the moment. Then it hit me.

"What? How do you know that?" I felt a stab of interest, but was unsure how the hell my sister had found that out already.

She shimmied toward me, shaking the bottle of formula and running her free hand from her face to her ass. "He never looked twice at me, and have you seen *me*?" she said in her most sultry, sexy voice.

I couldn't help myself. I was punch-drunk with tiredness. This whole situation was ridiculous, and I snorted a laugh. Then I pulled her close with my free hand and side-hugged her.

"Love you."

"Love you too, but seriously, the hottie is gay. He told me so."

"Yeah, right. He just came out and said, 'hey, I'm creepily watching my neighbor's house, and by the way I'm gay'?"

"Of course not," she said with theatric flair. Then she leaned in and fake whispered, "He came out and said he loved cock."

I covered up Mia's ear as best I could. "Don't use that word in here," I loud-whispered back, but she just laughed at me.

"Seriously, I explained that you, too, like cock."

I pivoted and left the kitchen, heading for the sofa and my quiet space, away from annoying sisters. The only problem was that she followed me. At least she brought my coffee with her and a plate of sandwiches. My stomach rumbled, and food sounded good right about now.

"All joking aside, he handed me a load of bandages, and I explained you were on your own here, and he told me he already knew that. But I might have added that you weren't in a relationship, and one thing led to another, and he said something like…" She screwed up her nose. "Being a single parent has to be hard, but being gay, if I wanted to have kids, I would have to blah blah."

"Blah blah what?"

"Oh, it was all..." She waved expressively, then reached for Mia. "Let me feed her, and you try feeding yourself, then you can both get some sleep. After I leave, I'll report to Mom that you are handling everything like a pro, and I can maybe get you an extra twenty-four hours before she decides your estrangement is something that she can ignore now that you're home."

"We're not estranged—"

"Don't even go there, Ash. She hasn't seen Mia since the hospital—"

"When she told me that I was holding her wrong—"

"She's a mom—"

"—and criticized that I was using disposable diapers."

She shook her head sadly, but Mom was always a hard thing for me to talk about.

Siobhan wasn't the child who mom said had *decided* they were gay or who had *chosen* to bring a child into an ungodly house. Nope, the one who'd done all that was me. It didn't matter that I'd explained everything, that I'd been born the way I was meant to be. Mom hated that I was gay, that I wasn't religious, and that I'd broken the worst rule in the Good Book. When I'd snapped one day and shouted that she thought lying with another man was worse than murder, she didn't say that wasn't true.

That had been the day I'd left for college, and since then, I'd seen her ten or so times on family occasions, and each time I'd left fuming. Siobhan still had a limited relationship with her, but that didn't mean I had to.

"So, changing the subject, what happened to my masterpiece?" She picked up an old blue ice-cream tub and tilted it so I could see the remains of the citrus yellow bowl she'd made me.

I held up my hand in answer. She put the container down and picked up bandages that were piled neatly on the counter.

Do I need them? What if Mia gets hurt? I should get bandages.

"Earth to idiot-twin? We need to get this cut covered."

I didn't argue as she passed Mia to me, who I held in my good arm. Then Siobhan wrapped me up like a mummy, making me feel as if I might never see my hand again.

"Mom says she would love to see Mia again, but she *understands* that it's difficult for you," she said, just when my defenses had lowered a little because she was caring for me.

My heart sank and I wanted to stop her from talking about mom because a whole load of crappy memories crowded into my head of years when Mom couldn't even meet my eyes, let alone talk to me. True, Mom had visited me and Mia in the hospital and a big part of me hoped she would have something profound to say— something that would mend the past. Of course she loved Mia, cuddled Mia, and she was my mom, so I was okay with her holding my daughter for the longest time. But when it came to the serious stuff, the part where she was supposed to say to me that I would be a great dad and that I had this, there had been nothing.

"She knows where I live. Not that I want her to visit." *Fuck, I sound like a heartless bastard.* I was just trying to protect my heart, and most of all Mia, because all I could imagine was Mia turning to her grandmother at age sixteen and explaining she was gay. Would she have the same heavy weight of disapproval thrown at her? Would she be told it wasn't God's way?

I had Mia to think about, and I didn't want Mom anywhere near her. That small window of opportunity at the hospital when Mom could have spoken to me and supported me had gone in the blink of an eye. How fucked up was that for what was supposed to be a mom/son relationship?

Siobhan glanced up at me and gave me the *stare*. The one that only a twin can give another—the one that gave sympathy and support while calling me on my shit. "Mom knows you don't want to see her, But I really think she understands it's her fault now; she's changed."

"She didn't seem changed in the hospital," I said, bitterly. "She was an awkward mess, couldn't look me in the eye, and didn't have anything positive to say to me."

Siobhan frowned. "The way she told it was that she tried to show you how to hold Mia in the hospital, and talked to you about diapers and that you shut her down."

"Jesus, sis. Let me remind you that she told me I was holding Mia like a football, and that disposable diapers are the work of the devil."

"She actually said they were the work of the devil?" Siobhan raised a single eyebrow.

"Something like that," I lied.

"Well, she thinks she tried."

"Tried? She never wanted me to decide to be gay. She never wanted me to have boyfriends. She never wanted me to have Mia." I was working up a head of steam now, but Siobhan pressed her free hand to my chest.

"I know, Ash. I know all that. But for Mia's sake, don't shut Mom out. Things have changed at her church, and... look, it's not my place to tell you what to do, but call her. For me? Maybe you can be the bigger man and extend an olive branch, okay?"

"Like I said, she knows where I live." We'd never gotten back onto a level footing. She'd never even met Darius, who'd been a long-term boyfriend. Not that she'd missed out there, because he was a grade-A dick. When I'd split with him but had decided to go ahead with the surrogacy, she'd been apoplectic. Although I'd only found out about that secondhand through a friend of a friend. It all went back to the church, back to her rigid stance on homosexuality and the whole thorny complex argument over what the definition of a family should be.

"You know she won't just visit on her own."

"Do you know what she said back when I told her my surrogate was pregnant?"

"Ash—"

"In the middle of one of her bible quoting tirades, she suggested the surrogate should lose the baby. Her own granddaughter."

Siobhan cradled my face and sighed.

"We all say things in the heat of the moment. Look at

my reaction over you not wanting to have me as your surrogate."

I winced at the memory. Mom was different. She was institutionally set on the fact that man-plus-woman-plus-baby was what a family looked like. We'd circled right back to the fact that I was going against God's law, or whatever she'd said after I'd shut down and refused to listen to any more.

"But Ash, you know she won't just drop in, not after you and her—"

"What?" I snapped, and she stroked my cheekbone with her thumb to calm me. It worked. Siobhan always knew what to do to stop my anger and anxieties fighting to surface.

"Mom didn't understand how beautiful your little family would be," she said. "How precious Mia is, but I honestly think she wants to. She just doesn't know how. So, what if you make her understand?"

"It's not as if she tries to listen to me."

"Maybe you need to be the one to build a bridge and help Mom to understand." Siobhan faced me, stood on tiptoes, then pressed a kiss to my cheek, "Because I swear, if *you* don't call and invite her by tomorrow, I'll lock you both in a room until you get through to each other."

I didn't doubt for a minute that was exactly what my stubborn sister would do.

"Why are you pushing this thing with Mom on me?"

"For Mia. Everything you do now is for her. That's just what being a dad is."

I closed my eyes briefly, and the sigh that left me

was full of a desperate need to make everything right for Mia. Siobhan had it easy, married to a man, a soldier, a hero, with two gorgeous children, a minivan, and a cat. She even had the ubiquitous white picket fence.

"I'll try and call her," I said after a moment's pause. Siobhan looked at me steadily, and she would see through the lie. "Okay, maybe one day you bring her over, and we can possibly talk," I added, and she relaxed a little.

We exchanged glances, and then she smiled at me. "I will always be in your corner, Ash," she reassured. "Now I need to go. I love you."

Mia and I waved Siobhan away. Then I closed the front door as all my energy left me in a rush.

One thing that could be said for my bratty, in-your-face, teasing, annoying sister?

She only wanted me to be happy, and through everything, she'd always had my back.

Unlike my mom who hated me and my baby.

SIX

Asher

With Mia in my arms I stared at my calendar.

"Wow, you're at day forty-five," I told the inanimate object.

It was the same calendar that I'd used to count down the days until Mia's arrival into this world, and now it marked each day that Mia had been alive. Each day in which I tried my hardest to be a good dad. That was all I could think as I circled today. "Not that I need to tell you it's day forty-five, because you're a calendar."

After I'd spent two minutes yesterday telling the sterilizer that it played an important part in keeping Mia safe, and explained how tired I was, it hit me that I'd begun talking to lifeless objects. Yesterday the sterilizer, today the calendar.

Neither had said anything in return, but I honestly believed that talking about things out loud was enough for me to make sense of them. I wasn't sure that I was ready to be sociable with real-life people.

Guilt flooded me, and even though I knew there was no such thing as guilt-free parenting, I wallowed in the feeling for as long as it took for the bottles to be done. I scooped Mia from her crib and sat at my desk, opening my laptop so I could try some of that multitasking that Siobhan had done so well. After a few tries at making Mia comfortable, I finally managed to log in, then opened my email. There was the usual content in there, a couple of contract emails that I dealt with first. I'd deliberately cleared the decks for three months so nothing would come between me and Mia's time, but there would always be the odd question. I owed my career a huge debt; without the payoff from one of my first game designs, I wouldn't have been able to afford over one hundred thousand dollars to go through the surrogacy.

After work mails I dispatched any spam. Finally, all that was left was an email from someone on the forum I'd signed up for, who was obviously stuck in the nineties by the state of the Hotmail address which was "nicholas.james.arthur.horner.7699210@hotmail.com." Firstly, not many people the right side of forty used Hotmail now, and secondly, did no one tell this person that shorter was better? I'd already formed an impression of the sender, as some tech dinosaur, and that wasn't fair. Not everyone was a computer geek like me.

I opened it, expecting the sender to laugh me off, something to make the loneliness worse.

"Let's see what they say, Mia," I said and shifted her a little when I noticed she'd stopped feeding and that she'd nearly finished the bottle. I placed her up on my shoulder, burp cloth in place, and rubbed her back as I read the email out loud.

"Dear Asher, welcome to Single Dads Together. I've given you access to the forum and sent a note to a couple of dads on here in a similar position to yours. It's okay to feel alone. I know I feel alone every day, and that is what we are here for. You indicated that you live on the West Coast, and we have thriving sub-groups from Seattle down to San Diego, so I hope you'll update your profile to be more specific, and in that way, you can find people in your locality who you can talk to. I'm here if you need help and my details are at the end of the email. I'm a father to three though, so it might not be an instant reply. You know what it's like to be a dad."

The name at the end was Nick. He lived in Del Mar, only half an hour's drive away. Was it wrong that I felt weird that this stranger who knew I was lonely lived way too close for comfort?

I followed the sign-in link in the email, changed my password once I was in, then scrolled to the forum subjects. This forum was as old school as Hotmail, but that didn't make the impact of what I was reading any less.

There was a chat group, and I opened up the latest thread, which dealt with sibling rivalry. Nick had started the subject, talking about a heated situation in a supermarket. I didn't post a reply, but the responses were even-tempered, useful, and everyone seemed super friendly and supportive.

I scrolled down other posts, and one caught my eye.

The Dating Game.

Nick had started that thread as well. It was about dating but more specifically about how, after five years, Nick was thinking of dating a friend from work.

It slowly became obvious that Nick had lost his husband five years ago, and that grief was only just ebbing enough for him to consider ever being with a guy for something more than a hookup. He had three children, twelve, ten, and eight, and he was lonely.

Some of the replies broke my heart. Stories of dads who'd lost partners. Some who said they would never love again. I had to click away.

I was looking for something on this forum, support, but also agreement that my ex was a waste of space and that I was right to do this alone. I couldn't read about other people's grief and not want to do something about it, and what did I have to offer in the way of help? Nothing.

I should have tried to sleep as Mia dozed on my chest. I was messing up any chance of refilling my energy tanks, but when the next post I saw was from a man called Tim in New York who posted an entire essay entitled, *lonely and alone*, I couldn't stop reading.

By the time I'd read the post and the comments and found my eyes filling with tears, I went back to my profile and added San Diego to my address, and my email contact. I wanted to connect with these guys because I was exhausted and needy, and I wanted to know I wasn't alone.

I couldn't help with their grief or their sadness or loneliness, at least not yet. But I could learn about these things, and somehow I would grow into someone who could help.

One day.

When I *finally* got sleep.

The forum was the first thing I thought about the next day. I reached for my iPad as soon as I had a spare moment and saw I had four emails from the forum. One was from a guy in Oceanside, a thirty-minute direct run north up the coast from me. His name was Brady, and he didn't seem to be able to get all his thoughts down in a coherent fashion. I could imagine him sitting there, desperate for a connection to some other man in a similar position. *You and me both, Brady.* He'd added his Messenger details, and I connected and left a short hello with an explanation of who I was. His icon was blank, so he wasn't online, but I already felt a kinship with him simply because we were both single dads. Then his icon turned green, and three dots bounced, indicating he was typing something back to me.

Brady: *Hi*
　Ash: *Hi*

I watched the dots bouncing again. They seemed to move for a very long time, and I imagined Brady at the other end thinking about what to write. Then they vanished, and disappointment coursed through me.

Maybe Brady had second thoughts about connecting with a stranger? I flexed my fingers, ready to type something, and then a long message appeared.

Brady: *I copy pasted this from a document, so don't think I can type this fast really. LOL. I'm going to be honest and tell you I have dyslexia, which makes using Messenger hard at times. I mix up things, and it takes me a while to get back to people, so apologies in advance. I use voice to text a lot, but you know how that works sometimes and then fails spectacularly. Nothing says stupid as when you type bank manager as wank manager.*

So, long story short, I worked out all of this to post to anyone I connected with in advance, and got a friend to amend and spell-check it. I wrote a couple of replies depending on who contacted me, and I had this one all ready to go if it was to another dad in the same position as me. Or at least a dad who is wondering about his place in things.

I'm really pleased you reached out to me, and I want you to know that even though I might not be able to type super-fast or make a lot of sense with what I write, that I would love to connect online to other people in my position. So if you don't mind me sending you messages that have short words, I'm happy to talk.

I care for two children: Lucas, who is eleven, and Maddie who is nine. Their parents, my sister and her husband, died some time ago now. In their wisdom, they gave me guardianship of the kids, so I'm both uncle and dad. It's hard but rewarding, and I love them, although they don't always love me. LOL.

A bit about me - I was working for a graphic design company, but it was impossible fitting work around putting Lucas and Maddie first. I do freelance drawing, which I have some talent in, and work hard to be a good dad, which it seems I have less talent in. So yeah, that's me. I'm twenty-eight, gay, and currently in a relationship with Robert, but I think he's about to walk out on me. I don't blame him. I don't have the time for him when he is home. Right now I think I'm losing him, so I'm feeling isolated and lonely because he isn't here, and I've never really had long-term friends. Not that you really need to know all of that.

Anyway, that is my story, and I'd love to connect if I haven't scared you off.

I reread his long post and then decided that I needed to take the plunge and connect with someone who was as lonely as I was. Particularly a guy who had a boyfriend who was at work a lot. When Darius had been doing that kind of shit, he'd been sleeping around. Not that I would say that unless this Brady person asked for my advice. Instead, I was all about reassuring Brady.

Ash*: Hello, Brady. I'm not worried about spelling or grammar, in case you're worried. I'm dad to Mia. She's only a couple of months old, but she's my everything. I write code for games. It's really nice to meet you. Ash.*

. . .

The dots bounced, and before I knew it, I was knee deep in a very slowly typed conversation with Brady about lack of sleep and grief.

Brady: *I'm line on in every evenings*

Although *on* and *line* were a little jumbled, I realized that somewhere along the way I had begun to pick up on the style of his writing.

Ash: *I'll hit you up tomorrow evening, then. Really good to talk.*

He answered with a smiley, which he did a lot through our online chat. I guess the cartoon images were a lot easier to work with than the mess of letters that made up words.

I sent him a smiling emoji back, along with a thumbs-up, and signed out of chat. Maybe we could meet up face-to-face one day, and *maybe* I could start to make friends outside of the ones I'd had through my ex who'd all vanished when he left me.

Two of the other three emails were general forum posts, and the last one was from Nick, who gave me the address details for a San Diego SDT group meetup, which was at his house.

Am I really going to go?

The address was thirty-two minutes away according to my maps app, but it would be the first journey I'd taken with Mia that wasn't us coming back from my sister's house. All I wanted now was email exchanges that confirmed to me that I was doing okay, so did I genuinely want to meet up with other dads?

What if those other dads told me I was doing everything wrong?

And what if they were right?

SEVEN

Sean

I *really* wanted to see Ash, to go next door and see if he was okay, which was just a thinly veiled excuse to see him. This was necessary after meeting his sister and having a weird-ass conversation that somehow ended up with me not only telling her I was gay but also agreeing her brother was hot.

That girl, his twin, had crazy mad interrogation skills. After the chat, in which it was explained very plainly that her brother was also gay, I had this insane idea that I might ask Ash out for coffee; a notion that wouldn't leave me alone.

So asking him out for coffee is what I *wanted* to do.

Unfortunately, what I *had* to do was attend the 6th Annual Trauma Awareness Expo and man the stall for Soledad Memorial Hospital. In fact, all three of us, me, Leo, and Eric were there. Leo and Eric in uniform, me in my scrubs.

Scrubs for fuck's sake.

It's how the public perceives the ER now, Sean. Suck it up sunshine.

Whatever. Scrubs *were* my uniform, and they were super comfortable, but it wasn't bling like my friends had going on. The fire department had brought a big shiny engine, and Eric was busy dealing with herds of kids and their admiring moms. Of course he was. He was a six-five, distinguished firefighter and could bench press who new how much.

Leo, handsome and slick in his dress blues had his police car, along with special dispensation to pretend to lock kids in the back seat and turn on the blue lights. Between him and Eric, they had the sexy first responders thing all sewn up. They were goddamn heroes.

And what did I have? I had Tracy from IT, who didn't want to be there, and an anatomically correct cross section of a human heart, with real pumping blood. Well, not exactly blood, but synthetic liquid that was leaking from somewhere and left my hands smelling of bleach.

"What happens if I poke it with a stick?" a kid asked me, all ginger hair and wide eyes, pointing at the fake heart. "Will that blood gush out all over me?" He couldn't have been more than ten, and there was no parent who appeared to be responsible for him. The last thing I wanted was for him to poke the expensive prop with the sharp, pointy stick that he was waving in front of me.

"Would you poke a real person in the heart?" I asked and nudged the display out of his reach.

"Only if they 'served it," the kid stated, and jeez, he

seemed as if he really meant what he was saying. Did we have a future serial killer on our hands here? I searched for Leo, and if I could catch his eye, maybe we could haul in the kid for questioning. "Nah," the kid added, "it was a joke." He peered at the table, at the pile of heart-shaped stickers with the hospital logo. "Can I have a sticker?"

"Sure you can." I picked up a sheet to peel off one, but he grabbed a pile of ten sheets, then ran before I could stop him. That was the most excitement I'd had all morning, apart from Tracy telling me in no uncertain terms that she was sick and that she had to leave. I offered to check her out if it helped, but she ran before I could catch her. Which meant I was now on my own, with the stickers, in my scrubs, and with a bleeding heart.

"You ever saved anyone?" another kid asked, this one maybe fifteen, the right age for my target market. I wasn't completely sure why I was even there—whether it was to sell the hospital services or encourage kids to concentrate on science more so they might one day become medics like me.

"I try and save a lot of people." I waited for a follow-up question.

"But not for real? Like from fires or from people with guns, right?" The boy stared right through me, and I was stuck in that awkward place between wanting to explain that I was one of those who tried to save the people after the disaster, or saying no and letting the kid move on.

"The stickers are lame." The boy picked them up,

then dropped them and left.

Yep, I was not manning what people would call the heroic-sexy stall at all. I wasn't a firefighter, I wasn't a cop, but I was the one who would attempt to mend these people enough to stop them from dying if they ended up in my ER.

I'm a quiet, understated hero. Obviously.

Eric looked my way, and I caught his gaze as someone took a photo of him with their mom scooped up in his arms. He winked at me, and I gave him the finger. Subtly of course; I didn't want to be caught on camera giving a firefighter the bird. The woman threw her arms around his neck, and it took two other guys from his engine to assist her from Eric's hold. That made me smile, and this time, it was my turn to wink at him.

The event was crowded, people spilling out of the tents, stopping, talking, some eventually worked their way over and asked me what I did. I explained I worked in the emergency room at Soledad Memorial, and got the same question asked in many different ways. For the older generation, it was questions about the television show. Was I like George Clooney in *ER*? Or *"You sure don't look like George Clooney in ER."* Then there were the ones who came over and told me all of their symptoms. By the time I'd dealt with my third case of possible hemorrhoids, it was two p.m., and I was done. The space in front of my table was so sparse of people I expected to see tumbleweed. The heart, which I'd named Henry, had somehow stopped pumping the fake blood, even though it was all plugged in to the portable generator. I was caught up in wondering if I should find a sharp stick and poke it when a commotion broke out in front of me.

"My daughter!" someone shouted. "Help us."

"Someone call 911!"

"She needs a paramedic!"

Then I heard Leo call my name, and I grabbed my medical bag, jumped the table, knocking Henry-heart to the ground and sprinting as best I could to where I thought I'd heard my name called. I recognized the woman; she'd been to the stall and spoken at length about her husband's diabetes. It was probably the only sensible conversation I'd had all day.

I slid to a halt and fell to my knees next to the young girl who was on the ground, foot bent at a weird angle, a cut on her forehead, and sobbing piteously. Leo joined me.

"Paramedics five minutes out," Leo said.

"There's bleeding," Eric added.

"What's her name?" I asked the mom.

"Becky," she said, and gripped her daughter's hand. "The bouncy castle is supposed to be safe, but she fell as she got off."

"Can you get me some room here?" I asked Leo and looked at him pointedly. This was a young girl on the ground, and a crowd of gawkers staring. Eric and a couple of his firefighter buddies formed a protective circle around us all.

"Becky? I just need to check your eyes, okay?" I flashed the light but everything was okay, pupils reacting as they should. The head wound was superficial, it was the ankle that looked bad. "And now I'm going to check your ankle as gently as I can, sweetheart." Leo cradled her head, and I examined the area. "It looks to me like it's just a sprain," I lied. She was already crying, no point in making it obvious it was broken. "The paramedics will take you to the ER and get X-rays." The paramedics arrived, and I passed on what I knew, adding quietly what I suspected about the break, and watched as Becky and her mom left. The drama was over.

The crowd of watchers melted away, and it was just me, Eric, and Leo in a circle.

"Now who's the hero," I deadpanned.

Leo snorted, but Eric frowned. "I have a bone to pick with you, *Doctor*," he announced and tugged me over to the big shiny scarlet engine. "Look."

All across the back, spelled out in the stickers I'd been handing out was one word. *ASS*. It was artistic, and I could make a good guess who had done it and that he probably had ginger hair.

Eric muttered as he peeled each sticker off, then patted the big rig. Any minute now he'd start talking to it. I sidled away, back to my stall, which was a little busier as people had followed me back, and I tried to fix Henry-heart, who now had a new hole.

"I'm not sure I can save you," I told the model and laid him on his side to stop the seeping scarlet fluid.

By the time volunteers from the hospital had dismantled our stall, the crowds had thinned, and those who were left were picking up trash and what looked like all the stickers I'd given out. I made a mental note to suggest that Memorial needed to rethink next year's marketing, and said my goodbyes. Leo and Eric were both on duty and heading straight out, but I was on day two of my time off, the forced break after working twenty-one days in a row. I left the care of Henry to the support workers.

Now, I could call a cab or walk, since I'd carpooled with Eric that morning, but I decided that even though I was in scrubs, I would walk home. It wasn't much more than three miles, right through the park, and I needed to enjoy the May sunshine while I could. All too soon I'd be back on the battleground at the hospital, although with a full complement of docs there now, maybe I'd even get more time off soon.

And pigs will fly.

The park was stunning, full of color and life, and I slowed my walk to an appreciative saunter, tilting my head up to the sun and feeling in that single moment that everything in life was possible. It was in that happy positive mood that I left the park, rounded the corner into our road, and spotted Ash collecting his mail. I quickened my pace to cut him off, glancing at his bandaged hand and noticing it had been redone.

"Hi, Ash," I said in my best neighborly way.

He blinked at me, and I could see he was working through his memories of who the hell I was.

"Oh, hey," he offered and then lifted his cut hand. "Thank you for the fix, if I hadn't already said. I mean, I probably said something, but right now, it's a blur."

"New babies will do that to you," I offered and was aware I came over as a combination of preachy and lame.

"My sister is visiting again," he said. "She told me

that her psychic twin connection told her I needed help."

"You have a psychic twin connection?"

"She says we do, but it doesn't seem to work from my end."

"Okay, cool."

"I should be in there."

I got the impression he was defending why he wasn't in the house with his baby. "She said I needed to let them have girl time for at least an hour. Do babies need that already?"

"I doubt it," I reassured. "At this age, all a baby wants is to drink milk, have hugs, and not have dirty diapers. Oh, and sleep."

"I have to go…" He began to walk backward to the house, and I went with him, desperate to connect. Why, I don't know, but there was something about him that meant all I wanted to do was talk to him and then maybe stare at him some more. He stopped just short of his porch and tucked his mail under his arm. "Do you know a lot about babies?"

"I know enough, but I'm an ER doc, not a pediatrician."

He sunk to the step. "I don't know anything about babies." He sounded lost. "We read all the books, or at least I did. Then I went to classes on my own, but none of it is working the same as what I read or learned. I have this schedule I made, from all the advice, and I pinned it to the fridge, about sleep routines and milestones, but I'm not following any of it. We had all these ideas, and now…"

I took his pleading look as an invitation that he

wanted to talk, and sat next to him. It hadn't bypassed me that he'd picked up on the use of the word *we*. Did he mean a boyfriend? Or maybe his sister? She seemed a pretty hands-on aunt.

"We?" I asked gently.

"My ex, Darius, and I, we started this journey," he let out a full body sigh, "but it was me who decided to keep going. He kind of left me holding the baby. But, not really…well, yeah I guess he did. Only having Mia in my life balances everything. I wanted her, I wasn't *left* with her."

"He doesn't know what he's missing. Mia is the perfect baby."

He shot me an amused look. "You wouldn't say that if you'd been the one changing her diaper last night. I've never seen anything that color before."

He shook his head ruefully, and I couldn't help but think just how damn cute he was.

"Diapers are hell," I agreed, and he smiled at me. Simply sharing that one small thing was another connection between us.

"The books never told me just how bad they could be."

"No book can prepare you for real life," I reassured him. "Things can turn on a dime."

"You sound like you're speaking from experience."

"Believe me, I am. When you're in medical school, you're told all kinds of things about procedure, about keeping yourself safe, but when it's hands-on in the ER, it's like battlefield medicine, so comfortable procedure flies out of the window."

He went silent and wrapped his arms around his knees, looking impossibly vulnerable, so much so that I wanted to hug him hard. After kissing him, of course.

"My sister is bathing Mia. Then apparently they might go and sit in the garden, and through that, I am supposed to sit and wait for them and enjoy the sunshine, or failing that, sleep."

"Maybe you should sleep."

He glanced at me. "I look that bad, huh?"

It was on the tip of my tongue to say that he might well feel exhausted, but he was sexy and hot. He actually ticked all my boxes, all dark and brooding, and with a runner's build. We were around the same height, and I imagined that kissing his plump pink lips would be worth taking my time over. Knowing he was gay just made everything much clearer. I loved babies, and it appeared that I was attracted to tired-looking single gay dads. I could get behind having some neighborly fun.

"She's only in town a little while, and then she's heading home."

His words broke through my appreciative assessment, right at the time I realized that him living next door would make hookups a disastrous option.

"Where is home for her?" I said to get things back on track.

"Near Pala. It's where I grew up."

"Not far then."

"No, an hour or so in the car, but her kids, my niece and nephew, are being looked after by friends because her husband, Dan, is overseas right now. He's military." He let out another sigh. "It's completely selfish, but I spent the first few weeks at her house, with her helping me to learn things, and she made me go home, so I'd learn, but she's come over because of the twin thing, and now, I'm scared for her to leave."

"I understand that."

"It's stupid how sorry I feel for myself."

"Hey, you want to know who lives next door to you?" I thumbed at my house. "There's me. I'm a doctor and can help you with all kinds of chills and fevers." His eyes widened, and I moved to reassure him immediately. "Not that your baby will get either of those."

"Mia, her name is Mia."

"Well, I happen to know as a doctor that any baby named Mia is immune from childhood illnesses," I deadpanned and actually managed to raise a smile.

"I'll remember that."

"Anyway, so you have me. Then there is Eric, who you met under difficult circumstances. He's a firefighter, a really strong guy, so he can come over and help you lift stuff, check your smoke detector, that kind of thing. He's also amazing at starting barbecues. Lastly there is Leo who is a cop, so if you have any issues, you can call on him, problems with neighbors, that kind of thing. He has a dog, Cap, named after Captain America, a black lab who eats everything in sight. So even after your sister goes, we can all be there if you need us, a ready-made first-responders unit right next door." A smile lit up his dark eyes, and my lust levels increased sharply. *He's gorgeous.*

Yes, he was a new dad; yes, there was a baby in there, but God, I wanted to kiss the man as desperately as I needed my next breath. Or at least touch him. All over. With my mouth.

I moved away a little in case my hands and lips got the better of me, but thankfully he didn't notice.

"I want this to work."

"Then it will. You should come over," I blurted because it seemed I had lost all of my game. Where was the interesting conversation and the detailed questions about him being a new dad? Or commenting on the story about the ex. Vanished, that's what. "Get a beer or something, meet the guys?"

"Maybe, when Mia has grown up and left home." He laughed at his own joke, and I smiled along with him.

The one insistent question I had inside me pushed to the front and wouldn't be denied. "So you and Darius, you're not together anymore?"

Ash scrubbed at his eyes. "God, no."

"Would you like to come out with me for coffee or something? A date maybe?"

Coffee. A walk. Some kissing. Sex. Whatever.

Ash huffed a loud laugh and stood, slapping his mail on his thigh. "Yeah, right. You're a funny man."

He shut his front door behind him faster than I could stand up. He thought I was joking? The thought of kissing him? Of touching him? Of all the kinds of hot and nasty things we could do together? I was hard and had to restrain myself from suggesting a date much more interesting and obvious than a casual coffee between friends.

I hadn't been joking.

EIGHT

Asher

"Was that Doctor Hottie from next door you were talking to?" Siobhan asked as soon as I stepped into the kitchen. She was stirring something that smelled like heaven, in a pot on the stove. Mia was in her rocker, and the music was playing low. I didn't dignify the Hottie comment from Siobhan, even though, yep, he was a hundred kinds of sexy and right up my street. Those eyes, and that layered hair a guy could get his fingers into, and those lips.

I could think a lot about those lips. Imagine I wasn't exhausted as hell and actually available and awake enough to hook up? I could go for Sean. I could lay him out on my bed and eat him alive.

No. Not on my bed. Mia is in my room.

The bigger spare room. No, that is where the nursery is all ready for Mia.

The smaller spare room and the single bed. Yep, I'll spread him out on that single bed, and then I'll kiss him and suck him, and I'll wait only long enough until I fall right the hell off the tiny bed and end up on the floor.

"Earth to Ash, come in Ash."

In my thoughts, I was still on the floor, with Sean the-hot-sexy-doctor looming over me, and it took me a while to refocus. Siobhan smirked. I ignored her and crossed to Mia and fussed over her as she stared at me. Her eyes were wide open, and I wondered if they would darken from the pale blue gray or would this be her permanent color. The egg donor I used had hazel eyes, I had brown eyes, but that didn't mean anything according to her pediatrician, because it seemed eye color was much more complicated than I'd been taught in high school.

According to the information, I had to wait between six and nine months to see for sure. I knew that because eye color was on my milestone list that was pinned to the fridge. What was gratifying about the list was that some things were checked off already. She had lost weight after birth, made the weight back, was holding my gaze longer, even though I knew I was still a blur. She was interested in the world around her, and I was sure if she could talk, she would say she loved a few things—like a fresh diaper, me rocking her to sleep, formula, and the fact that I was her dad.

I have to believe she loves that I'm her dad.

Eye color was only one of the exciting things I would find out about my daughter. She kicked her legs and caught hold of my thumb, instinctively closing her fingers around it and pulling it to her mouth.

"You don't want that dirty thumb," I warned and disentangled myself, pressing a kiss to her hair.

"Ash? Hello? Who were you talking to?"

"Sean. He was telling me all about my new neighbors next door, of which he is one, and it sounds like the start of a bad joke."

"Huh?" She turned from the stove and poured the saucepan contents into two bowls.

"You know like, a doctor, a firefighter, and a cop moved in next door."

She gestured for me to sit. I took the stool next to where Mia was, and grabbed a bread roll from the plate in the middle.

"Useful to have experts like that real close," she commented and dunked her bread into the rich, creamy chicken soup she'd dished up.

We subsided into silence as we both ate.

"Is it still okay for us all to visit next weekend?"

"Yes, absolutely."

This time she'd bring Evan and Debs, who were both excited to meet their new cousin again. I had the warm and fuzzies thinking about them with Mia, even though I knew Evan would still be pissed that Mia wasn't old enough to play computer games with him, given that those games framed his entire life. Debs, on the other hand, would be over the moon to have Mia to fuss over again. Which reminded me, the very next moment I was able to think about more than Mia and surviving without sleep, I really needed to get the bedrooms fixed up with new linen.

"There was a message on your machine," Siobhan

said when I'd finished my soup and drunk most of my coffee. The fact that she'd left it until after I'd eaten made me think it was a message I didn't want to know about.

"From Mom?"

"No, Darius."

My heart sank. As much as I had once wanted to hear him acknowledge that Mia was perfect and he was wrong to have left, I was done wanting to talk to him.

"What does he want?"

"I didn't play the message. I'm not *that* kind of sister."

I leveled her with a look, knowing full well she'd listened, and she bit her lip to stop herself from laughing. After a few moments of staring each other out, she sighed.

"Okay, so I listened. I couldn't help it. I was fielding calls in case it was Mom."

"That is the flimsiest excuse I've ever heard," I teased because I really needed to find lightness in this situation. At the end of it, a call from Darius never left me in a good place.

"Sue me," she said and then grew serious. "He wanted to know how you are, and said he was back in the States at the end of the month."

"Really?" Stupid, pathetic, soul-destroying hope swelled in my chest. He was coming home? To see me? And Mia? He would only have to take one glance at Mia, and he would fall in love with her, and maybe we could try again to be a family. I checked for the matching enthusiasm in my sister's expression, but there wasn't any. "What?"

"He's at a conference in New York, says you *have to* find a babysitter and you *have* to visit for some *fun times*." She did a good impression of Darius and his sometimes nasally, whiny, insistent voice.

My world crashed down again, as it did every time I let a tiny bit of hope back in my heart where Darius was concerned.

"Why do I not learn?" I said and scooped Mia into my arms. She'd become both a shield for me to hide behind and a reason to become a stronger man. "Can you delete the message?"

She shrugged. "I already did. Do you want to talk about it?"

I just wanted to be away from the kitchen and anything like sympathy from Siobhan, so I left, but she followed me, and we ended up standing in the hallway.

"Darius is a lying cheating selfish asshole, and he's not worth your pain," she said and hugged me and Mia close. Why did I think following Darius to San Diego was a good idea? I should have stayed in Pala. Even though my mom was in the same place, and even if childhood fears and insecurities plagued me with every turn I made. At least I'd have been near Siobhan.

I tried not to let any of this inner turmoil show on my face, but she was my twin. She *knew*.

"Look after yourself," she said with conviction. "You can do this, and we'll be here next weekend as we planned. I already changed all the bedding and put in a food order to be delivered, so all you need to do is make sure you try and get some sleep, and love your daughter."

Loving Mia was a given. Sleep, on the other hand, wasn't guaranteed. I selfishly wanted Siobhan to stay where she could help me navigate everything, but I didn't ask her. She had her own family, and with Dan away she was a single mom the same as I was a single dad.

I waved her away, standing on the sidewalk, Mia tucked in my arms, and didn't move once to try and stop her.

"Hi," a deep booming voice I recognized startled me. I turned to face the big drunken guy who'd woken Mia up the first night I'd had her home. He seemed taller, wider, and I must admit that even though he was smiling, I was intimidated.

"Hey." I tried for neighborly but began to take a few steps back toward the house.

"So I know Sean apologized for me, but I saw you out here and was thinking it would be good to explain myself to you."

"You don't need to do that—"

"We moved in when you weren't here, and the houses look so alike, and I was drunk because I'd had a bad day. Not that this is an excuse. We all have bad days..." He inhaled and exhaled noisily. This big man screamed capable and firefighter all in one pumped-up look, but his expression was vulnerable. I think he really expected me to be angry with him, but I wasn't. I mean, I had been on that night. I'd just gotten Mia to sleep, and this big oaf had caused me untold grief, but now, she was awake, happy, and I was in that mellow place that all new parents went to when everything was quiet.

"It's all good," I said with extra confidence in my voice in case he didn't believe me. "Thank you."

"No, thank *you*. If there's anything I can do for you, then you know where I live." He gestured to the identical house next door. The only difference with the exterior was that their house had a red door, mine was green, but once you got through the door, everything was different. My former neighbors were fond of entertaining, hence a pool, pizza oven, and barbecue set up in the garden, and the sound system piped through the entire house. But yes, from the front, it was easy to get confused if you were drunk and it was dark.

"I'll remember to ask if anything comes up," I said and went back inside, closing the door behind me and standing for a moment in the coolness of my hallway. Mia clutched at my shirt, and I looked down at her tiny mouth opening and shutting. That was my cue to feed her, burp her, change her, and then rock her while I checked work emails.

Or maybe I could skip that last part and instead go and sit in the shade in my yard and enjoy the warm day as she took her bottle.

Sounded like a plan, but my messenger showed a hello from my forum buddy, Brady, and Mia was asleep, so I decided to cradle her close, then stay inside and talk to someone who shared my worries about life.

Brady: *Hi, how you doing?*

Ash: *Okay.*
Brady: *Sounds bad.*
Ash: *Yeah, my ex contacted me today.*
Brady: *Are you still talking with him?*

I realized I'd begun to look at Brady's typing and understood some of the jumbled words, and I was translating them in my head. He would switch letters, and the sentence itself was disordered, but other than that, it all made sense, even to my sleep-deprived brain.

Ash: *God, no.*
Brady: *Can I ask you a personal question?*

That particular message took a long time to decipher, only because personal came through as peripheral, but it was long enough for me to go from wanting to say no, to wondering what Brady wanted to ask. I wonder how he read things. Was his reading of what I was saying just as bad as his writing?

Ash: *OK.*
Brady: *Is he Mia's dad?*
Ash: *You mean, is he the sperm donor? No. That is all me.*

. . .

Also, I was her dad, her *only* dad, and no one on this earth would ever take me away from her. I had a will, with guardianship passing to Siobhan, and legally Darius had no claim to Mia. I'd done this alone and had paid for every step. That was one of the single things that let me sleep at night on the off chance Darius had a complete about-face and demanded access.

Brady: *That's good, then.*
   Ash: *Yeah.*

We chatted about other things, baseball of which he was a fan, and our shared love of superhero movies, and when we signed off, I had a smile on my face. I really wanted a friend.

   And Brady was becoming the friend I needed.

NINE

Sean

Beer in one hand, chips in the other, I hovered at Ash's door. Eric had said he'd seemed friendly this afternoon, but I'd seen his sister leave, and maybe he was lonely right now.

I was only being a good neighbor by coming over and checking on him.

Yeah, right.

I knocked softly, thinking that if he didn't answer, then I would go home. The last thing I wanted to do was to wake Mia up if she was asleep, or worse, wake Ash up as well. I'd almost given up when Ash opened the door.

"Hi," I said immediately. "Thought you might like some company."

"Uhmmm," he began and shot a look behind him.

"I can only stay an hour, and I won't be drinking. I'm on shift, but I'll share the Doritos with you." I rustled the bag and waited.

"Come in," he murmured and stepped back from the

door. I went inside, marveling again at how two identical houses on the outside could be so different inside. Whereas ours was a real bachelor party house, this one was more sedate, elegant even. I saw a wood burner in the front room that I glimpsed as we passed, along with two solid leather sofas. Everything in this place was understated but quality, and it smelled of baby powder. I placed the beer down on the counter, along with the chips.

"Coffee?" he asked, and I nodded.

I expected him to have beer, but he had the same as me. Maybe beer wasn't a good fit for a single dad who was fully in charge of a child. Next time maybe I'd bring over some fresh beans for his complicated coffee machine.

"You want to go into the garden room? It's tidier out there."

I glanced around his kitchen, which, to my eyes, was clean and organized. The only mess was a pile of laundry on the counter and a box of unopened diapers by the kitchen door. I knew better than to comment though because one man's mess is another man's empty space. So I followed him to the glass-roofed addition and wished we had something like it next door.

Mia was there, in a portable crib, waving her chubby hands in the air and staring up at a Disney mobile.

"You like Winnie the Pooh?" I murmured as I crouched next to her. "This is Winnie. He's an extraordinary bear. Once he ate so much honey that he got stuck in a rabbit hole—it's a lesson in life, baby girl." I swung the mobile. "And this is Tigger. He's a funny dude, and he has this bouncy tail you'll love." I went round and told her about Eeyore, Kanga with tiny Roo, and last of all, Piglet. "Piglet is my favorite," I informed her, in all seriousness. "He's a shy little thing, but he's super brave, and cute." She caught my thumb and held it tight, and I looked up at Ash. "Can I hold her?"

I'd seen a lot of things in the ER, complex things, tragedies, uplifting moments, frustrating cases, life-changing seconds, but there was nothing like a baby to make me smile. One day, I would have children of my own.

"Of course," Ash said after a moment's hesitation. I bet he was sitting there contemplating all the ways that he could say no. And why wouldn't he? After all, he didn't really know me that well.

I scooped her up, then settled on one of the comfy chairs, nestling back and sitting Mia on my chest.

"Hello, beautiful, hello you." I crooned and bounced her.

"She smiled today," Ash was proud. "For real, not a reflex smile but a real smile."

"Did you smile, baby girl?" I asked Mia and bounced her again. "What a clever thing you are."

I caught Ash's stare and returned it head on. He held the look for a moment and then shook his head and turned to pick up his coffee. I'd caught him in some kind of thought at that moment. *I wonder what it was?*

"Do you have a lot of babies in the ER?"

I hesitated before answering. I had babies with nowhere else to go, I had babies born on the streets, I had babies that were hurt, but I wasn't going to tell him that.

"Some." I picked Mia up and pressed a kiss to her nose. "But none of them are as gorgeous as you. No, they're not." I was using that voice that only an adult thinks is cute, but Mia didn't seem worried, and I swear I caught the hint of a smile.

I settled her in the crook of one arm, letting her hold my thumb, then expertly placed her back in the bassinet and clicked the button for the mobile to move. Then I sipped coffee and opened the Cool Ranch Doritos. Multitasking with food and drink is something all ER personnel became good at. I put the coffee down, working my way up to what I wanted to say, a mouth full of chips. Should I explain that sometimes when a person is tired, they may not understand what another person was saying to them? Should I say that the offer of a date was a real one, and it wasn't often I asked someone out, and that I was more the casual hookup kind of guy, but that Ash was different?

I stuffed in another handful of chips, then passed them over to Ash, who shook his head.

"No, not with coffee but thank you though."

I stared down at the coffee in one of my hands and the Doritos in the other. "It's gross, isn't it? At work, you eat what you can get your hands on in the spare seconds you have, and you get used to all kinds of weird combinations. Cupcakes and cold fish sticks with half-defrosted stew, canned corn, followed by burnt chocolate toast, you name it. I've tried all the food combinations under the sun."

He smiled at me, and I felt emboldened.

"I wasn't joking, you know," I blurted.

His smile wavered momentarily, but he hid it behind his coffee mug. "Sorry?"

"About the date. I think a date would be good."

He blinked at me and opened his mouth like he was going to talk. Then he shut it again and appeared confused.

"You. Me. Coffee. Outside?"

"I have a baby," he said and sat back in his seat as if that much had cost him all his energy to say.

"I never said anything about it being just me and you. Bring Mia. Anyway, it would be a second date," I added and waited for him to fall into my trap.

"Huh?"

"We're doing our first date now." I lifted up the packet and rattled it. "Coffee and Doritos, me, you, and Mia."

"That's not—we're not—no." He sounded confused and in denial, but my time was nearly up.

"I need to head out to work." I stood, he stood, and we were about as close as we'd ever been. I could actually reach out and touch his face. "So, when will we have date two?"

"I'm tired," Ash said. "I'm a new dad. I don't have time to—"

I reached out and took his hand, and he didn't fight me, so I tugged and drew the hand to my lips and unfurled the fingers to press a kiss to his palm. Then I folded the fingers back in, and he let out the softest of sighs.

"You can keep that one for later," I kept my tone soft, then gave him a cheery wink and left the house without a backward glance. He hadn't pulled his hand away, his eyes were wide with astonishment or desire, and I was so going to take it to a real kiss next time. I was on and off shift a lot over the next few days, plenty of time to take things super slow.

When I got home, I barely made it into the house before letting out a whoop of excitement. Cap yelped and ran out to find me, growling, then leaping at me in a doggy attack of fur and licks. I went to the floor, and we roughhoused for a few minutes before Cap got bored and wandered off to the kitchen.

I lay on my back, staring up at the funky light fitting that changed colors. We'd lost the remote for it the day we moved in, even though the owners had left it for us on the kitchen counter with a note. The LED was stuck on red, and that thought made me smile.

Everything made me smile. Ash may not have known it yet, but we were going to have a date.

TEN

Asher

I settled into a routine, or at least as much of a routine as I could have with a newborn. I definitely did not think of Sean and his stupid-ass hand-kissing nonsense. Or the claim that we'd had our first date.

So what if the kiss he'd pressed to my skin was one of the most erotic things that had ever happened to me. So what if he was cute and funny and ate his Doritos as if they were going to be ripped away from him at any moment. And did it count that he held my daughter in such a gentle and confident way, and that he was right? Mia *had* smiled at him.

What didn't help was that lying in bed that night, just thinking about the kiss to my palm was enough to make me smile *and* make me hard.

I was *not* going on a date with Sean because he was too dangerous to be around. I could fall for a guy who kissed my hand and treated me as if I was special.

Yep, way too dangerous.

So I avoided him if I saw him, which was only twice and from a distance, and everything settled back to normal.

By the time Tuesday came around, I was sleeping when Mia slept, dealing with life when she was awake, and I felt like a god. I still checked her breathing all the time, and every move I made in the house was because of Mia, but I did manage to catch up on some television with her dozing on my chest, and I even solved a coding problem for the beta launch of a new game I was part of. All one-handed, which made for slow coding at first, until I realized that the sling I'd bought for the long walks in the park was actually useful to hold Mia close *and* give me two hands to type.

She loved it. Or at least I imagined she did because she didn't cry and even fell asleep in there, and to me, that was a win. Of course, I was kind of hunched over and finished the session with a tension headache and sore shoulders, but yes! I *could* do this single dad thing.

Brady*: You there?*
　Ash*: Yep. Feeling good today. In control.*
　Brady*: Take the day as a win.*

I was going to, and the feeling lasted until the evening.

The first sign that things were heading south was that Mia wouldn't drink her milk. She batted at the bottle, screwing her face up in indignation that I would even think she might want it. She had this cry I'd identified as

"I'm pissed at you, Dad," and that was the one she was giving me now. Sobs and hiccups turned to wailing and then fitful sleep and then more crying.

My short-lived time of being the best single dad on the planet subsided with her sobs, and then when I thought I might have finally had her down for sleep just before three a.m., I brushed a hand over her short fluffy hair, and her skin felt warm.

Or was that me feeling cold? *This is San Diego. This is June. I'm not cold.*

All the knowledge I had about fevers fled my brain, and I fired up my laptop. What did I Google in a situation like this? I knew that body temperature fluctuated, depending on the baby, on the time of day, on their age. I went straight to my go-to page of the American Academy of Pediatrics and picked up the thermometer to check. The ear thermometer was the best I could buy, based on a hundred positive reviews and recommendations on all kinds of baby forums from people with more experience than me.

I checked the display, then referred to the website. "99.4. Okay, Mia, body temperature for a healthy baby is in a range between 97 degrees and 100.4, so you're not too high." I checked again. "99.7, shit, Mia." Had the reading really gone up point three in the few seconds? One more check and Mia mewled in protest. "99.3. What do I do?"

I picked up my phone and thumbed to Siobhan, but was this something I should've been asking her about in the middle of the night?

She answered on the third ring, just as voicemail was going to click in.

"Ash?" She sounded wide awake.

"Were you awake?" I asked.

"No, but getting a call from someone in the middle of the freaking night wakes me the hell up."

Guilt flooded me. She might have thought it was Dan calling from overseas or bad news from the army or from me. *I'm shit at this.*

"I'm sorry—"

"Whatever, Ash. It's okay. I wasn't properly asleep anyway. So what's wrong?"

"Mia is hot."

"Okay," She stayed calm, even as I was freaking out. "How hot?"

"99.4, then 99.7, then 99.3."

"Okay, how long between those readings?"

"A couple of seconds. So why are they all over the place?"

"You need to… when you use an ear thermometer if you don't get it placed properly, it can sometimes… I told you that you needed to buy a rectal one. Look, none of that is important. Does she seem ill to you?"

"She's crying a lot."

"Okay, well, it's probably nothing to be super worried about, but how about you go and check with Doctor Hottie."

"What?"

"You know, Doctor Hottie from next door, see if he's home, go and ask him, and he can say if you need to go to the pediatrician. Phone me back. Let me know, and, Ash? Don't panic. This is perfectly normal."

I didn't stop to argue that temperatures all over the place was anything *but* normal, and that Mia was hot, and that I was *fucking panicking.*

I wavered between going straight to the hospital or doing what Siobhan suggested. Maybe I should do both? If I knocked on the door, and Sean wasn't there, then I would put Mia in the car. I dressed quickly and then wrapped Mia up, then unwrapped her because she was hot. Then enfolded her back in the blanket because she was hot to the touch, but that didn't mean she was *hot.* She was already in her sleeper, and a tiny jacket, a hat on her head.

Then I headed next door, just as a car pulled up onto their driveway and parked. The door opened, and a streak of dark shape headed straight for me, a dog dancing around us and nosing at my leg.

"Cap, heel," a voice said from the darkness. "Sir? Is everything okay?"

The man stepped out of the shadows, and he was in a dark blue uniform. The cop, Luke or something. No, Leo, his name was Leo.

"I need to talk to Sean," I blurted. "It's my baby."

Leo didn't hesitate. He unlocked the front door, stepping inside, the Labrador winding its way around his legs and trying to trip him up.

"Cap, kitchen," he ordered, and after a few short barks of disapproval over the fact that he wasn't allowed to stay, the lab padded into the kitchen and sat glaring at me. "I'll get Sean." Leo took the stairs three at a time, and there was banging, crashing, cursing, and then Sean appeared at the top of the stairs, buttoning jeans and attempting to get his arms through the sleeves of his T-shirt, all in one flailing mess of movement. He bounded down the stairs, coming to a halt next to me.

"What's wrong?"

I thrust Mia at him. "99.4, 99.7, 99.3," I said in a manner that wasn't an explanation at all.

"Rectally?" he asked, and I balked.

"No."

"Okay then," he turned Mia, and she hiccupped. "Let's have a look then." He stalked away from me, avoided the dog, cut through the kitchen, and into what seemed like a storage room where, in my layout, there was a small office. The room, lit by a bare bulb, was piled high with boxes. "Sit here," he instructed, then vanished, only to return carrying a big bag. Sean opened it one-handed and pulled out petroleum jelly and a thermometer, laying both on the table, then began to take off Mia's clothes one layer at a time.

"Was she in her crib?" he asked as Mia caught his thumb.

"No, I was working, and she was…" I patted my chest. "In a sling."

He nodded as if maybe he'd had a eureka moment, and took off her sleeper so she was just in a diaper. Then he felt all over her body and didn't seem worried by anything. At last, the mewling stopped, and he smoothed his finger over her head. I pointed at her torso, which had a faint speckling of red.

"Oh my God, is that a rash?" I panicked. "Do we

have a glass to roll over it? She could have meningitis. They said we should watch for that—"

"It's okay. It's just a heat rash," Sean said. Then he glanced up at me. "She wore a diaper and was dressed in a sleeper, jacket, and hat, in a sling against your chest. Right?"

I counted off the items in my head. "Yeah."

"I think maybe she was just overdressed." Sean picked her up, and with one hand, he held her still, talking nonsense to her, until the last of her fitful movements stopped and she relaxed against him.

"You *think* she was overdressed?" That wasn't a diagnosis. I couldn't help her with the word *think*.

"Feel her now."

I touched her forehead, and she didn't seem as hot.

Then it hit me. Hard. "Are you saying that I caused this?" I began evenly. "I made her overheat? This is on me?"

"Ash, you couldn't have known that—"

"Oh my God, I could have…" All the energy in me fled, and I slid down the wall. "Someone needs to come and save her from me."

Sean sat next to me, tilting his knees so that Mia was propped up. She was so little in his gentle hold, and I'd never thought just how tiny she was next to an adult. Small, vulnerable, and I'd hurt her by over-caring. She was wide awake, her cheeks not as red, her head cool to the touch now. I took her from him, feeling ashamed of myself, angry at fucking up, and unreservedly humiliated.

"Don't beat yourself up. You did the right thing

when she started to get hot," Sean said and knocked his knee against mine. "You have the most precious thing in your life in your hands right now, and you love her more than anything. You were trying to care for her, and when something seemed wrong, you came to a doctor."

My cell vibrated, and I pulled it out of my pocket, responded to Siobhan's *Everything ok?* with a *yes, it's all good. The doctor checked her out X,* then pocketed it again. I'd have to deal with her teasing in the morning, but right now, I had a doctor to face and embarrassment to deal with.

"Come on," he cupped my knee in encouragement. "I'll walk you home."

"You don't need to, it's okay." I stood and picked up the discarded clothes, taking the blanket and putting it over her shoulders, then taking it off, before standing there like an idiot and feeling awkward.

Sean placed the blanket over her with a light touch. "Trust yourself," he murmured, and for the longest time, we were so close that it was almost as if he was Mia's other dad, and we were intimate in our love for her.

That thought startled, me, and I left their house faster than I thought possible. Mia slept five hours solid.

I didn't sleep at all.

ELEVEN

Sean

It was Friday, and it had been three days since I'd seen Ash with Mia and her overheating. Not for want of trying, though. I'd double-shifted at the ER, then on this, my first real time at home, I'd spent an inordinate number of hours outside, on both front and back yards, simply on the off chance I might see him, but the closest I got was seeing his scarlet car as it disappeared down the street about an hour ago.

"Explain to me again why you're sitting out here planning a way to accidentally meet up with our neighbor," Eric said from my side. He was at home today and had decided his current mission in life was to follow me around like a shadow.

"I just want to make sure Mia is okay," I explained again.

"Nope, still doesn't make sense," he said and sat heavily on the front step of our covered porch. "He lives next door, dude. Knock on his door and ask him if she's okay."

"I can't do that."

Eric side-eyed me, then huffed. "Maybe you want to ask him more than just whether Mia is okay."

I glanced at him in time to see his eye-roll.

"What else would I want to ask him?" I asked, even though it was a moot question because I knew I wanted to ask him out for another coffee or *something*. Eric understood me far too well not to see this for what it was.

"You found out he plays for your team, and you wanna take advantage of him."

Eric made a kissy face, and I punched him in the arm, hard. He laughed at me because he was made of stone, and my weak-ass punch wasn't going to even make him flinch. At work, they called him Tree, but Leo and I refused to call him that. He'd been Eric ever since we were kids, and that was the name that stuck.

"Well, if all you want to do is ask after her health and you're not interested in his fine body, then maybe I'll go over and ask him out for a drink?" Eric held my gaze, but the three of us had rules, and I'd explicitly stated that I'd called dibs, even though it had been Eric who'd seen him first.

"It's three. Don't you have somewhere to be?" I asked and waited for him to realize that he should get a wriggle on not to be late on shift. He stretched a little, then ambled inside; that was Eric, the gentle, laid-back giant, the one who was rarely ruffled.

Apart from when he lost people he wasn't able to save.

When he came back out, in a uniform that was snug

over his broad chest, I waved him off and then went back to sitting on the step and passing the afternoon by. Not waiting for Ash. Not at all. I wondered if I should invite him and Mia to our house for a meal on my next evening off. *Yeah right, a whole evening off. That's likely to be in a decade's time.*

When his car turned back into the road and he parked on the driveway, I was striding over before I could even think what I was doing. He spotted me as he opened the door to get Mia out.

"Hi," he sounded wary.

"How is Mia today?"

He couldn't quite meet my eyes. "She's good. Thank you."

Yep, it was one of *those* conversations where we were going to be polite, so I grabbed the bull by the horns.

"I'll buy you a coffee in the park if you like?" I said in that offhand nonchalant way that wasn't fooling either of us.

He leaned in to pick up Mia, and I imagined he was giving himself thinking time.

"I can't do *coffee*," he said with all the emphasis on the word as if he was implying it was something more. Which it was, but I wasn't going to give away my endgame yet.

"I've seen you drink coffee." I smiled at him.

"It's nice you invited me, but I'm a new dad, and I don't have time to invest in dating." The words were clearly rehearsed as if maybe he'd sat in his beautiful garden room and thought up what he would say if someone asked him for a *coffee*. I could work with that because all it meant was that he'd thought about the coffee, and that was a win for me.

"It's not a date, just a drink, and maybe cake." I smoothed my fingers over Mia's downy head, marveling at how soft she was and how tiny. Of course I'd seen babies before. I'd delivered my share of them in the ER, and I had nieces and nephews, but this was different, and for the life of me, I couldn't work out why. "We can go now, Put Mia in a stroller. Do you have a stroller?"

He couldn't quite meet my gaze. "I have four," he mumbled.

"Four? Strollers you mean?"

"One tiny baby-sized, one for rough terrain, one for the car, and one for when I go running." He tilted his chin as he waited for criticism.

Instead, I picked on the easiest one of those. "You go running?"

"No, but I might. And before you say it. I know we live in a paved road, but in the canyon, it's rough terrain. She is tiny right now, but she'll get bigger."

I held my hands up in mock defense. "I wasn't going to say a thing. A parent can never be too prepared."

I could've told him stories of teenagers coming into the ER with stomach cramps, not even knowing they were pregnant or being deep in denial—there were no signs of any kind of strollers or similar preparation in cases like that.

"Exactly." He seemed to warm to my agreement.

"So? Coffee?"

He opened the trunk and pulled out the stroller,

laying it on the ground, and then in a couple of deft movements, one-handed, he had it up and clicked into place. I should have offered to hold Mia as he did this, but he seemed adept as if he'd been practicing, and I honestly felt like at that moment I might scare him off. He intrigued me—there was a story behind his deep brown eyes, and I wanted to know more. Why was he a single dad? Where was his support network? Other than his sister, I'd seen no one. Were his friends giving him space with the baby? Did he have friends? He tucked Mia in with blankets from the car, expertly hooked a large changing bag onto the front, shrugged on a backpack that looked heavy, and then locked up the car.

"Okay, then," he announced. "Coffee."

We left the street in silence as we worked out who was walking where on the sidewalk until we reached the park entrance and there was room to walk side by side.

"How are things going?" I asked as I stepped over a discarded branch that showed distinct chew marks. This park was dog heaven, and when Mia grew a little, she'd have a wonderful time in here. Maybe she could play with Cap. Or maybe Ash would get her a dog. Who knew?

"She had a weigh-in and checkup, and everything is good. Her weight is good, I mean."

"She's a strong baby."

"So far."

He sounded as if he expected there to be things that went wrong, and I wasn't in a position to disabuse him of that notion, given the things I'd seen. Still, I hated to hear his hesitation and wished I knew exactly what to say to make him smile.

We stopped for a moment as a group of school-kids marched across the path in sets of two, being corralled by three harassed teachers. One of them waved at me, and I smiled. Mrs. Ferris was one of those teachers who inspired and whom everyone loved. It was she who'd persuaded me on the first day we moved in to come to the school and talk about hospitals, with subjects ranging from injections to guns to drugs and everything in between. I'd done my first visit at the end of last week and enjoyed it and had persuaded Eric to go next. Mrs. Ferris actually lived a few doors down from us, right next to Gina Lazar of tuna casserole fame.

"Sean! Hello!" she called, and the entire class of six-year-olds broke lines as everyone clustered around me, Ash, and the stroller.

"Is that your baby, Mr. Sean?"

"He can't have a baby!"

"He so can. Mom said so."

"Mr. Sean! I lost a tooth!"

"Mr. Sean, is that your boyfriend?"

"My mom says she wants to marry you!"

"Barney pulled my hair!"

"I saw a squijjle."

"It's a squirrel, dummy."

"Get lost, fart face."

"She called me fart face!"

Everyone talked at once, and Mrs. Ferris waded into the fray. "Children, that's enough."

It seemed as though every one of them wanted a

piece of me, but she soon regained control and hurried them away with a meaningful glance that she threw at me and then to Ash. I laughed and shrugged, then turned to joke with Ash, who, instead of smiling, was pale and unsteady.

"Mia will be that age one day," he blurted. "I can't be a dad to a six-year-old. I'm barely hanging on to being the dad of a baby. Mia will hate me. What if she thinks a squirrel is called a squijjle and nothing I say will change her mind. She'll go to college, and everyone will laugh at her calling them squijjles, and it will all be my fault. I don't know what I will do and…"

I stepped into his space, a little closer than would've been entirely comfortable for him, and he reared back. Still, it had the desired effect because the panic subsided in an instant. That was something I'd learned when I was a resident, and it never failed me. People were so lost in their own panics that they built a circle around them in which to freak out, and me stepping inside it would throw Ash.

"What are you doing?" he asked, but he couldn't step away any farther, because he was right up against the small white fence that bordered the path.

"Count back from twenty," I said, and he focused on my voice. "C'mon, twenty… inhale, exhale, nineteen…"

"Eighteen… seventeen…" He counted down, separating each number with a breath, and as each one passed, he seemed less panicked. In fact, he swayed toward me. Either that, or I was swaying toward him. Only a few inches separated us, and I could've leaned forward to get my first taste of his tempting lips. Just one small kiss. "... one," he finished and closed his eyes. "Sorry."

"You're entitled to freak out every so often," I murmured.

He moved imperceptibly closer, and I felt the puff of his breath against my lips. Just a couple more inches, and we could kiss, but if we did, what then? He'd warned me he wouldn't agree to a second date, and here we were, about to kiss.

Or not.

Ash wasn't some hookup that I could fuck and forget. This was my neighbor, and it scared me that I was so impossibly attracted to him.

"We should get coffee." I was torn between talking and kissing, but I had to stay focused. Maybe I was imagining it, but I thought I saw disappointment flicker in his expression, but he smiled and huffed a laugh.

"Industrial strength, please."

"I'm on it," I said, and the intense moment passed before we headed for the café. I casually checked the rise and fall of his chest. At least he wasn't panicking anymore.

We sat at a table with the view out over the small pond, ducks floating in the water, and it was a while before we talked. I was happy to let him guide this, and after moving the stroller so that Mia was in the shade and then fussing with the small blanket, he sat back and took the first sip of coffee, sighing and closing his eyes.

I still didn't interrupt what looked like an orgasmic experience between man and coffee. The expression on

Ash's face was enough for my cock to begin to fill, as the thought of seeing that face while we were in bed—

"Can I have some cake?" he asked.

I blinked at him to get my head out of the scene I'd been building in which I was buried inside him. "Cake?" I asked. That was a stupid question because yeah, the image of what we could do in bed or on the bed or the floor was difficult to chase away. I couldn't remember the last time I'd felt such an instant attraction to anyone. He indicated the plate with the chocolate cake on it, and I felt so stupid.

"Of course. I bought it for you."

"Thank you, I'll buy next time," he assured me and forked up the first mouthful. The way he closed his lips over the morsel, then chewed and sucked before swallowing, the tip of his tongue darting out to collect a stray crumb, meant I went from half-hard to erect in an instant. I had so many questions I wanted to ask. Then I latched on to the perfect conversation starter.

"So, you and your sister look a lot alike."

He smiled ruefully. "She's pretty."

"So are you." *Fuck. Did I say that out loud? Who the hell calls another man pretty?* Me clearly.

He looked at me with skepticism. "Do you often call men pretty?"

"Not really, well, maybe."

"Eric said you did."

"What do you mean?"

"That first night he thought I was one of your hookups and that I was 'pretty enough.'"

I took some time to answer.

"Just because pretty is used in a gender-specific way doesn't mean I don't find things pretty." I leaned in. "I think you have gorgeous eyes and a pouty, sexy, kissable mouth and chiseled cheekbones and a strong jaw, and I want to kiss you."

"Oh," he offered after a pause. Well, that wasn't the most amazing of responses, and I'd flashed my hand there with what I was feeling. *Way to fuck it up, Sean.*

"Sorry."

"Don't apologize." He forked up another mouthful of cake. "I'm actually flattered, what with being too exhausted to even look in a mirror, let alone shave."

How did I tell him that the rough stubble and the way his hair fell around his face meant he was even more like sex on legs? I had no game today, and there was no easy way to say any of what I really wanted to say, so I changed the subject.

"Tell me about Mia?" I peered into the stroller and bopped her nose with my finger, not enough to wake her up but enough for her to move a little. She was so cute, all in pink, including a soft hat that shielded her eyes.

"What do you want to know?"

Ash sounded cautious, and I wasn't sure if that was because he thought I would criticize his choices or whether I was plain old nosy.

"You know that I was with a guy and that we started the journey together. Only he didn't make it this far." He pushed the now empty plate away from him and brushed at crumbs on his shirt. "What else do you want to know?"

"Was it hard to find support?"

He shrugged, but his sad expression betrayed him. "You know what it's like. When you want to start a family and you're in a"—He paused then air-quoted the rest—"... nontraditional relationship."

"The longest I've dated anyone was David in my senior year, and that only lasted a month, and there was no expectation of a family, so I probably don't know as much as you think I do. I should imagine it's impossibly hard."

"Yeah, as I said, there was supposed to be an *us* doing this," he murmured and looked right at me. "Darius was loose with his affections, but he proposed when he was drunk, and I think he loved the idea of it all, even though I knew he'd been seeing this other guy. But I couldn't bring myself to say yes and overlook his shitty behavior. I should have known there and then that I didn't really love him, that I was just in love with the stability and supposed support. I said no to marriage at that moment because we were too involved in the surrogacy thing. He said he'd changed his mind about having a baby and marrying me, then announced he was moving to England for work, all in the space of a few minutes. It was only after he left that I learned there had been two other men he'd slept with and that he'd been unfaithful to whatever relationship I had in my head from day one."

"Ouch."

"Yeah, well, the career opportunity was too big for him to refuse apparently, and he said he'd come find me when he was back, even though I told him it was over. Only, after three months, he decided he wasn't coming back, actually the day before I got an email saying the latest egg had taken and everything was a go. I was the sperm donor, so he had no connection to any of it, and in the best possible way everything fell into place. When I called him to talk to him about it, he said he was sorry. That was it. Just sorry that the baby was nothing to do with him, and he was done with it and that I should have a nice life. He was sleeping around, messing me up, and I honestly thought I was in love. How stupid was that?"

"It's not stupid to want to be in love."

He glanced at me and nodded. "Anyway, now you know why I'm here doing this on my own." Then he tilted his chin in defiance as if he expected me to have something to say on the matter.

"It's no one's business, least of all mine, what kind of family you've created."

He inclined his head in thanks. "Now I'm a new dad, and I had to change my plans, but I had money put aside, finished whatever contracts I could, and so far, it's been exactly as I imagined it would be. Exhausting, exhilarating, and rewarding, and it fits in with my career, which is freelance video game design."

"I'm impressed."

"You're impressed with me? Jeez, you're a doctor. It's me who is impressed."

Our gazes locked, and something passed between us, a mutual attraction, a spark of something that left me fully turned on but buzzing with questions. Only, he beat me to it.

"Is Eric your boyfriend?" he asked in one big hurry,

as if the question had been sitting on the tip of his tongue.

I couldn't help the snort of laughter that escaped me. "No, God no, he and Leo are my best friends, and we share the house. There was one moment way back when Eric and I thought it might work, but one kiss and we were stepping away scrubbing at our lips. Brothers always, lovers never." I laughed then, recalling that day when we'd thought one easy way to fit dates in with job training schedules was to do each other. It had been an interesting but ultimately horrific debacle.

"I met Eric the other day. He's bigger than I remembered from the puke-in-my-shrub incident, but he also doesn't really look like Vin Diesel. I mean, he has hair and everything." He covered a yawn with his hands.

"He started going gray when he was fifteen, and he's embraced the fact, even though Leo and I never fail to tease him. He's a firefighter, big and strong, but he's a teddy bear once you get to know him. You should meet him socially. And Leo."

"One day," he murmured.

Inspiration hit me. "Wait, I have an idea. All being well, the three of us are off-shift on Tuesday, and we have some stuff to do, but then we were thinking of firing up the grill." I lied about the grill part, but I did know for a fact that all three of our schedules had given us a rare day off together. Typically, on any day where our shifts lined up to give us space, we went out volunteering at the local kids' home as a team, carrying out handyman-type maintenance, but after we did that, we could *then* fire up the grill. "You and Mia are welcome to join us. You could meet the guys in better circumstances." He looked uncertain, and I sweetened the deal. "And Cap the dog as well."

"It will be difficult though with Mia."

"In what way? Timing of feeds? We can work around you."

"No, that should be… but you know she's a baby, right?"

"Well, yeah."

"What if she cries?"

That's what's worrying him?

"Nothing that the three of us can't handle," I reassured him. "Come over about three? I have a shift starting at seven that evening, so we'll eat early. Is that okay?"

He nodded and was distracted when one of the pond ducks waddled over to us. I wanted him to write everything down about coming over so he didn't forget, but the duck was far more interesting it seemed. Anyway, I was just next door, so I could pop over and remind him. Or leave a note.

If he doesn't come over, then I'll get the message that he doesn't want to be friendly with his neighbors. Or me specifically.

I needed to find my mojo where attraction was concerned. Too much work, too few hookups, zero relationships, and I was rusty for sure. Not that I'd forget how to kiss a man, particularly not one as gorgeous as Ash. In fact, I could've kissed him there and then. It wouldn't have taken much. I could've moved closer, reassured him that even if he was an exhausted single father, I found him far too attractive not to want to kiss him.

The duck quacked indignantly at something that a duck would find important. Probably the fact that we had nothing to feed it.

The sound was enough to make Ash jump. Then he smiled at me, looking a hundred kinds of embarrassed.

Jeez, he had one hell of a sexy smile.

I couldn't help it. I leaned forward and brushed a kiss on his lips. He looked startled, and I felt smug and happy.

I could kiss that smile each day and enjoy every minute of it.

TWELVE

Asher

Ten minutes before we were due to leave to go over to Sean's house for food, I was completely organized. We were only a few steps from the house next door, but I'd packed for the apocalypse. I had a pacifier, a backup pacifier, and a further pacifier in the changing bag. Not that Mia even seemed to like pacifiers much. I had burp cloths, two changes of clothing, a changing mat, diapers, wipes, formula, a hat for shade, one for warmth, blankets… you name it, and I had it, all packed up on the stroller, which nearly toppled over. My thinking was that Mia could sleep in the stroller when she was tired. I'd reached the front door before I realized I was missing the most important thing.

Mia.

I stood for a moment in my hallway, with my eyes closed. What kind of dad packs all the peripherals and forgets the baby asleep in her crib? My chest tightened, and I breathed my way down from twenty, just as Sean had shown me when he'd gotten so damn close I could smell the citrus of his shower gel. Or shampoo. Or whatever.

All I knew was that he'd smelled good, and for the first time in what seemed like forever, I'd been hard. I could have swayed even closer, mesmerized by the clear blue of his eyes. I had a serious thing for men who exuded the kind of confidence that Sean projected. The way he'd held Mia, the way he walked and talked, his sense of humor, his close friendship with his two housemates, all came together in one appealing sexy package.

Don't think about the word package.

Would he kiss me again? Deeper, harder? I was hoping so while at the same time wondering what the hell I was doing even thinking about it.

I ran up the stairs, slowing as I entered my bedroom and the scent of Mia hit me hard. Only this wasn't talc and love. This was a diaper filled with contents from hell itself. I couldn't help it. I gagged and reached for one of the clean sleepers to put across my nose so I could get closer.

"You need to deal with this first," I said out loud.

It was everywhere, her back, her legs, soaking through her sleeper, and there was nothing for it. I took off the clean T-shirt, my best one, and my jeans, and then, in my underwear, I lifted her from her crib where she lay eyes screwed up, a wail moments away. Then the two of us went into the bathroom, and to the changing table I'd pushed into one corner. I stripped her and made a quick decision that the sleepers was going into the garbage with the diaper and almost the entire pack of wipes. At least she didn't begin to cry, and by the end of it, she was staring up at me with her beautiful wide eyes, like I hung the moon and stars.

Still in my underwear, I got into the shower with her in my arms, and we showered together until we both smelled of baby shampoo and sweetness.

"How can one tiny person make so much mess?" I sang to her as I dried her off and left the bedroom window open to get rid of the lingering smell before bundling up the bedding and throwing it into the wash. Dressed and ready to go again, we were now forty minutes late, but at least she was clean.

I couldn't see Sean when I arrived, but that didn't mean anything. Because their house was on the corner edge of our road, their garden was three times the size of mine and full of bushes and plants. All I could see was the sparkling water in their pool and the barbecue manned by the guy who had vomited into my bush, and the cop from the other night.

"Hey!" the cop called.

I sauntered over, giving myself enough time to remember his name. I remembered I had a way to recall his name, and that it had been something very clever, but I'd forgotten the reminder thing, and nothing was coming to me.

"Leo," he introduced himself and held out a hand. "And you met Eric, right?"

Eric shot me a grin, then concentrated back on the burgers he was flipping. The scent of them was awesome, and the idea of a bun filled with burger and onions and ketchup had my stomach rumbling in anticipation. I had managed breakfast today, but other than that, it was only coffee holding me together.

"Ash," I replied, then shook his hand and Eric's.

"And this must be little Mia?" Leo asked and held out his hands in that age-old demand to hold the baby.

"Yeah," I said and tried to ignore the unspoken request.

"Can I hold her? I love babies."

After a moment's consideration, I passed her to him, my hands not leaving her until he had her secure in his hold.

"Mind her—"

"Head, yeah, I'm used to this. I have six nieces and nephews, and I'm godfather to five of them."

"Six?" I couldn't get my head wrapped around any of that; Leo must've been the same age as me, and his siblings had managed to produce six kids?

"I'm the youngest of four." He rocked Mia and murmured soft words to her, and after a while, I tried to let myself relax.

"Beer?" Eric asked and held one out to me.

"No, thank you. If I drink, I'll fall asleep." I laughed at my own joke, anything to deflect the fact that I didn't want to drink until Mia was eighteen, or maybe thirty. I wanted to be there for her whatever she needed, and I'd grown up in a house overshadowed by a father whose downtime had been as an unconscious and unwieldy weight in an easy chair. *I won't be that dad.*

Eric nodded, and it was obvious that he approved, and I had no idea why, but that reaction mattered to me.

"You made it." Sean came to a stop next to me, carrying a covered salad and his own beer, grinning widely.

"Yeah, sorry I'm late. There was an incident."

Sean placed the salad and beer onto the table next to the grill and held out his hands for Mia.

"She's all mine," Leo protested and turned his back on Sean. "You've already had your go." Then he began to murmur to Mia again, "It's my turn to cuddle you, isn't it, Princess Mia? You want to stay with the hero cop, not the stinky blood and guts doctor." He took a seat, well away from the barbecue, and placed her on his knees, tickling her tummy and letting her grip his hand.

"You've lost her now," Sean said with a sigh. "We all have. Leo's a baby magnet."

"Not to mention the baby-mommas," Eric pointed out. Then he inclined his head to me, "And baby-daddies."

I let out a weak laugh, one that I hoped underscored my current unease that I wasn't the one holding Mia. Then I tried to pull myself together. This was a trip out, this was socialization and included food that wasn't cereal, and mostly these were three capable guys who seemed to be genuinely friendly neighbors.

"How long have you lived in your house?" Eric asked.

"Three years now. We bought it when we first started looking into surrogacy." I realized the slip of including Darius in my description and decided to head the questions off at the pass. "To be fair though, my ex didn't ever live here. He had a place in LA where he spent most of his time." In hindsight, it was obvious that I had been the nest builder, the one who'd wanted a real home to bring a baby to. I'm not sure Darius ever wanted a home, and that was on me for pushing my expectations onto him.

And for him never telling you what he really wanted.

Although would I have listened, even if he had said he wanted to stop or told me he didn't want to start a family in a three-bedroom house in the 'burbs? I always thought I would have, but I'd become so fixated on what I wanted I'd never even known he'd been sleeping with other guys or that he'd been searching for work overseas. I mean, how far does a man need to run to get away from me? London, England, it seemed, and now, according to his profile updates on Facebook, he was on vacation in Bali.

"But it's just you now, with Mia," Eric stated this as fact more than a question. I nodded, and he slapped a burger onto a bun and handed it to me. "Well, you have us to help if you need us. I mean, I owe you one for sure. Anyway, onions and relish and the entire contents of our cupboards is there, courtesy of Sean, who does nothing by halves. Don't give anything to Cap," he added and pointed at the black lab fast asleep under the table. "He ate an entire bag of buns and is in disgrace."

I took the burger to the table he'd pointed at, which was groaning under the weight of about ten different bottles of ketchup and mustards, along with a big bowl of warm cooked onions I decided to ignore for now. My mouth was watering, but I just needed to do one thing.

"Are you okay with Mia?" I asked Leo, who waved

away my question and continued singing his mash-up of *Jack and Jill* with what sounded like a Justin Bieber song. Whatever he was creating had Mia staring at him, kicking her legs and waving her chubby fists. So I did what every new parent did when they get five minutes peace. I inhaled the burger as if I was never going to see another meal, then sat back in my chair and let out a deep groan of satisfaction. I glanced up to see all three men staring at me. Eric was smirking, Leo smiling, and Sean? Well, Sean seemed weird, his face scrunched up, his eyes narrowed, and he wasn't moving at all.

Eric cleared his throat. "Sean, are you sure I can't ask Ash out for a—?"

"No," Sean snapped. Then he gestured to the pool. "Come with me, Ash, and I'll show you the pool."

Should I tell him that I can see the pool from my house? Or that when the house had been vacant, I'd volunteered to take care of said pool and had used it on more than one occasion? He looked so intense that I said nothing and instead padded after him, stopping when I could see the pool but could also glance back at Mia on Leo's lap.

"Anytime you want to use it, feel free," Sean said and waved at the clear water. It wasn't hot today, not San Diego summer hot, but it was warm enough that I'd have loved to have been diving in. "Eric teaches swimming sometimes, so when Mia is big enough, you could ask him to teach her. I know he'd do it. Not only that, but obviously he's trained in first aid if anything happened… shit… I didn't mean to say that. What I meant was—"

"It's okay. I know what you mean. You're reassuring

me. People do that a lot. Only they bring up all kinds of new worries." I was teasing, but Sean seemed concerned, so I punched him in the arm because hey, that seemed like a good idea at the time. "Joke," I added and wished I wasn't so lame.

He examined me as if he was studying me under the microscope and took a step closer to me.

"Eric likes you. He told me that if I didn't do something, then he wants to ask you out."

"What? He does?"

"So I need to do something."

He was so close I could see the darker blue around his pupils. "Okay."

"You can stop me if you don't want me to kiss you," he murmured, his voice as soothing as the one Leo was using to talk to Mia.

"I want you to kiss me," I said.

He reached out and cupped my face with one hand. "You have the most beautiful lips," he growled.

I was hard. Even with everything that weighed me down, the worry, the diaper thing, my mom, the world, this moment crystalized as a single perfect thing.

"Are you sure?" he asked, and I sighed with impatience.

I swear if he doesn't kiss me now…

The first press of his lips to mine was chaste, a brush of something so soft I barely felt it, and he pulled back. I lost myself in his sapphire eyes and waited for another one. I didn't have to wait long as he cradled my face in both hands and tilted my head to kiss me again. This time he didn't hold back, and I parted my lips, desperate for a taste of him. He licked into my mouth, our tongues tangling, and I rested my hands on his biceps before sliding them down his arms and resting them on his hips. He was just the right height for me. He wasn't pushy or toppy or waiting for me to call the shots. We were together in this kiss, and I don't think I'd ever been kissed so thoroughly before. I wanted to touch him, to pull him against me and feel if he was as hard as me, and when we broke for breath and I opened my eyes, I saw lust in his expression, and I dove straight back in.

I slipped my hands around to his ass, cupped him, tugged him close. I could feel his cock hard and pressing against mine. He groaned, and I was powerful and unstoppable and so damn needy. We moved. I moved, or he did. I don't know, but the need in me for the touch of a man, this man, was overwhelming. I lost myself in kisses. Nothing mattered, not the sun or the water or the fear over Mia or…

Mia.

I eased myself away, and he chased me for the kiss, eyes closed, only opening them when I let go of my hold on his ass.

He smiled at me and pressed a finger to his lips.

"Wow," he murmured.

"I need to…" I thumbed back at Mia and waited for him to argue about how Leo had her and it was fine and that just like the rest of my life I should pull my head out of my ass and get things into perspective. He didn't say any of that.

Because he's not Darius.

"Let's eat some more," he announced and followed

me back to the circle of chairs, rearranging himself in his shorts. I just thanked the heavens that my cutoffs were structured denim and that my loose cotton T-shirt was untucked and long. Cap was up and snuffling around the table holding the relishes and curled up next to me when I sat down.

I didn't give him any burger.

Well, I did, but it was the tiniest bit ever, and no one saw me. Maybe one day I could get a dog, something to make the house seem more like a home. Mia would love that, I was sure of it.

By the time I'd finished my second burger and fed Mia, I chilled out and listened to Sean, Leo, and Eric teasing each other. They'd clearly known each other a long time, as evidenced by the fact that they'd all lived on the same road as kids.

"So my mom bought me a medical kit for my birthday," Eric said. "You know, one of those little ones with the stethoscopes, and I decided, at the age of five, I was going to be a doctor."

That would have been fine coming from Sean, but it was Eric, the firefighter, who'd stated that fact.

"So what happened?" I asked.

"Sean demanded I swap my kit for his firefighter dress-up clothes, and that was it, my entire life shifted."

"Eric cried," Sean said and saluted Eric with a beer. "I remember he was all 'waaaaahhh, I want my baby medical kit back.'"

"I was traumatized," Eric said and fake scowled at Sean.

"It shows," Sean teased.

Leo cleared his throat. "Then aged seven, I arrived on the scene, with my dress-up cop outfit, and we'd play first responders. It was kind of cool."

"Except I was always the victim," Sean said. "Eric wanted to rescue me from impossible situations, normally up trees, and Leo wanted to pretend arrest me. We never got to play the bits where I used my fake scalpel on them."

The banter continued for a while, and I didn't feel left out. I felt as if they were including me in their little stories about how they all, as seniors in high school, decided what they wanted to do with their lives.

Eric went straight from school into the fire service, Leo got a criminology degree and then joined the SDPD, and Sean was saddled with huge college debts and had spent most of what he called his youth, studying for exams. They'd stayed friends through all of it, and when it had come time for Sean to look for a residency, he'd come home, shared a shitty apartment with his two friends, and worked his ass off at Soledad Memorial.

"The house is mostly Eric's," Sean explained. "But Leo and I are happy to sponge off him."

"Whatever," Eric gestured and pointed at Sean. "You both invested and own twenty-five percent, and you know it."

"Yep, we own a quarter of this bachelor paradise," Leo added and fist-bumped Sean. They struck me as being as far from typical bachelors as possible. Although I guess there was still time for the wild parties to start, and I held hope that they wouldn't be the kind of neighbors a person ended up hating.

When Mia stirred from her dozing, it was six, and Sean had to leave for the hospital, but he walked me out and didn't stop until we reached my front door. I stepped into the cool interior, and he followed me and shut the door.

"I just want to kiss you goodbye," he said and cradled my face again.

This kiss was awkward as I was still holding Mia, and we were sideways on, but still… this man could kiss. When we parted, he pressed a small touch to Mia's head, then opened my front door and let himself out. He winked and waved, and then he was gone, and I was all alone in my house. My belly was full, I'd had a good afternoon in the shade, and once Mia was fed, inevitably the two of us would fall asleep in the garden-room.

Sean was there in my dreams, not in an erotic cock-waving kind of way, but in a gentle lovemaking way, the kind that left me breathless with the kisses. When I opened my eyes and the last of the dream drifted away, I carried Mia up to her crib and lay back on my bed.

I was like a kid after a first date again.

And it felt good.

Ash: *My next-door neighbor kissed me.*
Brady: *?*
Ash: *He's a doctor, a good guy, and he kissed me.*
Brady: *Tell me more.*

So I did.

Saturday came around all too fast, and with it, the arrival of my sister and her kids.

"Uncle Ash!" A whirlwind headed straight at me, and even tired, I managed to turn in time to scoop up my niece. Debs was nine, but she wasn't too aloof to cling to me like a monkey to a tree. I hoped that she never would be.

I hugged her hard before setting her down. "Debsy!"

"Hiya," she announced and swung around me to peer right in my face. "Didja hide Mia?"

"No, she's right there, but she's sleepy," I warned, and Debs kissed her gently on the head.

"I'll give her more kisses after she's awake," she announced, and I didn't stop her as she opened my secret cupboard. In it, I kept all kinds of bad-for-you snacks. Coming to Uncle Asher's place meant free access to choose one thing from the cupboard. She selected a Twinkie and disappeared up the stairs. I knew where she would go. I had a bookshelf in the smallest of my two spare rooms, filled with books for her.

She was my niece, and I loved her and her brother, Evan. I felt the same pain in my heart when they were upset as I did when Mia cried, with an intensity that ripped me apart. Maybe it *was* a twin thing? Maybe there actually was a physical connection through Siobhan to the kids. Whatever it was, they were Siobhan's children, and I loved having them in my life. It was seeing her with them that had made me crave my own children. When people had said to me it must be wonderful to be an uncle, they were right, but I wanted more as well. I wanted to give Evan and Debs cousins who would love them unconditionally. I wanted to build our family.

Evan followed at a more sedate pace, headphones in, and gave me a fist bump. Twelve going on twenty-one, he was a dude who didn't like to show the world anything but his coolness. He helped himself to chips from the secret cupboard, then sloped off to the stairs, heading up with a muttered, "later," and then it was just me.

"Now don't kill me," Siobhan started as she came into the kitchen.

I grinned at her. "Why? What did you do?"

She stepped to one side, and someone else came into the small space. Someone whom I was meant to call but didn't, and someone I didn't really want to see right now.

Mom.

I picked Mia up from her rocking seat and held her close. Nothing my mom could say was going to touch Mia, because I refused to let it. I wanted to cover Mia's ears and run—I'd never felt the flight reflex so keenly.

"Oh," Mom said and placed her handbag on the work surface, crossing to peer at her newest grandchild and blocking me in a corner. "I forgot she was so beautiful."

I bristled at her emotional statement. What right did she have to make any comment at all?

I caught Siobhan's gaze over Mom's head and glared at her, and all she could do was shrug as if she was saying I should deal with it. Dealing with my mom was the last thing I wanted to do.

"Uh-huh," I said and tried to ease out of the blocked area.

"Can I hold her?"

"She needs a nap," I said and sidestepped Mom to take Mia upstairs and put her in her crib. I checked in on Debs, who was surrounded by a pile of books, found Evan in the nursery playing games on his phone, and finally I had no reason not to go back downstairs.

Mom was waiting for me in the hall, and Siobhan was hovering at the kitchen door.

"It's so good to see you," Mom said.

"Why are you here?"

Mom glanced from me to Siobhan and back, then with steely determination, she straightened her spine and tilted her chin.

"I wanted to see my granddaughter."

I had so much I could've said to that. About how she'd never wanted me to have a daughter, or how she didn't want me in a relationship with another man, or hell, that she'd accused me of choosing to be gay. All the hurtful stuff piled into my head, but I wouldn't give in to the pain. I wanted Mia to know her family, but not the hateful side, not to hear that I was less of a man or that I couldn't be daddy to my little girl because it wasn't God's way.

"You can't walk in here and expect a damn thing," I said.

She winced, and again, we were at an impasse, and the room was growing smaller around me.

"I'm sorry," Mom said, to break the silence. "I don't know where to start, but for the things I said in the hospital, I'm sorry."

What? What did she mean sorry? "It goes back further than the hospital. Like when you told me right at the start that you hoped the surrogate lost the baby."

She was stricken. "I didn't mean it to sound like that, I swear. I only said that God would show us his intent—"

"Enough with your kind of God. Not in my house, Mom."

"I was wrong, and I want you to forgive me." Mom sounded desperate.

"Now? You come here now and say that? I love you, but you hate me—"

"You didn't make it easy for me to love you—"

"What the hell, Mom?"

"—but I couldn't ever hate you, Ash, please."

Siobhan moved between us. "Mom, go and sit in the garden."

Only when Mom walked past me slowly and headed outside did I let out the curse that had been wedged inside me. "How could you bring her here now? I didn't say you could bring her—"

"I told you if you didn't call her I would."

Anger knifed inside me. "You know why I don't want to see her—"

"Go for a walk; get some air." She sat on the third stair up, a gatekeeper of sorts. "I'll keep an eye on Mia. Come back in a bit; think about what you want to say."

"I don't want a damn walk."

"Go, get that air. Then come back, and we'll talk, rationally."

"But Mia—"

"I'll look after Mia. Mom is in the garden—"

"Are you saying I'm a child who needs to cool off?"

"No, you both need to get over the fact I brought her with me. Now, the kids are okay. So go."

I toed on my sneakers and closed the front door behind me. I got as far as the bushes in the yard three doors down, where I had a good view of my house, and I waited. I should go back, look out for Mia. Why was Siobhan saying me and Mom should talk? Why was that so important?

I wish I knew.

THIRTEEN

Sean

I'd been out for a run when I rounded the corner and walked straight into Ash. When I say run, it was more of a fast walk and nothing more than a mile, but I felt fitter today than yesterday. Kind of.

"Hi," I said and couldn't help but notice that his dark eyes were framed by the thickest lashes and that he had a small scar over his left eye. How had I not noticed the scar before? Or his lashes? Then I realized he wasn't returning my smile.

"Siobhan made me go for a walk. She said I needed air. I thought Mia needed air, not me. I'm thirty-one. I'm a grown-ass man, but she just looked at me and told me she was fine with Mia, needed me to calm down, and that I needed to get air."

"Okay—"

"She just turned up with Mom, as if I'd invited Mom or something. I didn't invite her, and then Siobhan looked at me and told me I needed air. What if Mom goes up and holds Mia when I'm not there?"

Wait? Someone needed to supervise a grandmother's visit? What wasn't Ash saying?

"Sisters like to tell you what to do." I shrugged. My sisters were prime examples. They would come over to our old place, the apartment I'd shared with Eric and Leo, and tidy up after us, tutting and talking under their breath. It was way better than when Leo's mom had come over and decided to call in a priest to banish the devil when she'd found a half-empty family size pack of condoms next to her son's bed.

We hadn't needed a priest back at the old place, we'd needed a fumigator and for the other residents to stop being so damn noisy.

"They do?" Ash was so damn serious, as if my answer might solve an ancient riddle or something.

"And they *over* care."

He frowned at my words. "I call it interfering." He blinked. "At least I think I do. What if something happens with Mia when I'm not there, and who the hell needs air?"

I didn't answer what was clearly a rhetorical question, "So are you going to stand here and get the air, or do you want to go for a walk?"

He stared at me, and I could tell he was still on edge and probably just as exhausted as he'd been before. Then he glanced down at me in my running shoes, and his eyes widened.

"Did you run?"

"Yes. No. I mean, I walked fast." I turned from him and took a few steps toward the park. "Come on, let's go."

He didn't follow, so I circled back behind him and shoved him a little—this dude needed help. I didn't check out how nice his ass was in his slim-fitting jeans or the way his shoulders were broad. Nope. No staring at all.

When he finally began to walk in a straight line, I walked next to him and guided him straight to the café on the edge of the park and pulled out a chair, encouraging him to sit.

"Coffee?"

He nodded and pulled out his phone, typing away furiously, and when I caught myself thinking how cute he was, I had to check myself. He was tired, stressed, and needed coffee. I could do that for him, and with the twenty I had in my running belt, I bought coffee, with cream and sugar on the side, along with toast and jelly, and a slice of chocolate cake. I could always eat anything he didn't want. I could lean over and kiss him as well, and I wanted to, but he seemed so serious. He put his phone down and fell on the coffee as if it was heroin and he was a junkie searching for a fix. Maybe I should hold him back and tease him with it…

Mmmm. Restrained. Restraining Ash, having him all tied up with nowhere to go and all spread out for me. What a good idea…

I ignored my treacherous libido, even though I couldn't take my eyes off the way he filled out his T-shirt. He had the body of a runner, tall, slim, strong legs, but he clearly lifted weights or something because he had muscled arms. I could appreciate his form without getting myself involved in sex fantasies.

Honestly, I could.

"That's good," he near-purred, and the pornographic sound went straight through me, and my body stirred and got itself all wound up. Not great when I was wearing running shorts—thank God they were a size too big for me and loose around the groin.

"Here," I said and pushed the plate of toast toward him.

"Is that for me?" He was adorably confused.

Not helping.

"It's difficult to get time for yourself with a new baby," I explained and nudged the plate again. He picked up a slice of toast and bit off a corner, closing his eyes as he chewed. "Air is good."

"I had Cheerios this morning," he mumbled as he brushed crumbs from his mouth. "Or was that yesterday? What day is it?"

"Saturday."

"Right, of course, Siobhan is here with the kids." His eyes widened as he recalled something else. "And Mom."

"It will be okay," I reassured, then sat back in my chair and sipped hot coffee, watching him over the rim of my mug.

"I know it will. One day it will work out either way, and I'll settle into being a dad."

I leaned in. "A hot, sexy dad, whom I want to kiss right now."

"Oh."

"That kiss we shared was incendiary."

"I know." The tip of his tongue darted out to dampen his lips, and I *really* wanted to kiss him now.

"Can you imagine what we'd be like together?" I dropped my voice so no one else could hear, and he leaned in to me.

"Uhh…"

"You were so hard."

"I can't. I want to, but…" He shuffled in his chair, and I could tell the moment that reality forced its way into our moment. "I should be back at the house. Mia might need me." He stood from the table and held on tight to the back of his chair as he swayed. I didn't even consider staying and letting him leave alone, even if that slice of cake was appealing. He seemed even more tired than he had been at the cookout, and I wondered how much sleep he was getting since the temperature scare. I scooped the cake into a napkin, and together we headed home as I picked off bits of chocolate and walked at the same time.

He quickened his stride as we exited the park. "I need to go in there and ask my mom why she's here." His stride became a jog, and I nearly lost the remainder of the cake as I kept up with him. "Sorry, I have to go," he said and darted down his drive and across the front lawn, fumbling with a key and bursting into his house.

What I wouldn't have given to be a fly on the wall right now. I wondered why he was worked up over his mom, and imagined any time where my parents and I would be on the outs. I couldn't think of one.

Cake finished, I ambled along the path to my house and let myself in. Cap was at the station with Eric, who often took him in to be the firehouse dog. Leo was on shift until morning. It was just me on my own until I had to report for work at ten p.m., aka nightshift hell. So I only had myself to please, and I thought a swim was in order. The pool, a complicated design of interlocking circles along with a Jacuzzi and a longer part where I could actually swim short lengths, was the sole reason the three of us had bought this place. It was perfect, and given we all loved swimming, plus this being balmy San Diego meant that it would get a lot of use this summer, I was sure. Slathered in waterproof sunscreen, I headed outside in my swimming trunks, sunglasses on, and a new thriller on my Kindle. I had five hours to kill. I was full of cake. I carried a beer with me. I was set to go.

This is the life.

FOURTEEN

Asher

The door slammed back on the wall, but I caught it before it rebounded and smacked me in the face. There was no sign of Siobhan on the stairs, and I ran up them two at a time to my room, heard a sound from my bedroom and followed it to the source. By now I'd worked up a head of self-righteous steam.

Mom was crying.

I stopped in the doorway, my eyes going straight to Mia, who was fast asleep in her crib, and there was that awful second where I thought something was wrong. But Mia was breathing, snuffling a little in her sleep, and Mom was still crying.

Not huge heavy sobs, but silent tears, staring down at her hands, her fingers laced together. My anger fled in an instant, and my heart ached. There had been too many times I'd seen her in tears. When we'd lost Dad, Siobhan and I had only been ten, and I'd seen my mom cry so much over him. She'd loved him, but I don't remember loving him at all. Then there had been more tears when Siobhan had fallen pregnant with Evan, more at her wedding, and then when Debs arrived. She'd cried when I told her I was gay, but for that, she'd railed at God for letting me make unwise choices. I should be hardened to the tears, but I wasn't.

"Mom? What are you doing up here?" I stepped into the room, and she looked up, startled, dashing away tears. Had she not heard me come into the room?

"Siobhan said—"

"Well, Siobhan shouldn't have—"

"Please, Ash."

I crossed to the crib and stroked Mia's soft hair, subtly moving so I was between Mom and her.

"You should let her sleep," Mom said, then bit her lip as if she regretted saying a thing.

I sighed, but it wasn't the sound of a man who was put upon or desperate to avoid his mom. The unconditional love a son has for his mother had ended the day I'd approached her cautiously to explain I was gay. That was the moment she'd announced it was wrong.

That I was wrong.

We didn't talk much after that, and soon enough I'd left home for college. I didn't go back home on any vacation time, working on my off days, hooking up with guys, but most of all being honest with myself in all things. Mom had tried to contact me, but the few times we talked had ended up with me having to justify why I was gay. She refused to believe me in all things to do with sexuality.

Moving out young had been on her list of things her misguided son would do, and she'd said to my face that she expected me to end up stripping to make money, or worse. In her opinion, the East coast where I was going for college was a dangerous place for people *like me*, and when she'd fallen back on using evidence from Scripture to back up her decisions, I would always walk out.

Don't date girls, don't date boys, don't date anyone, study hard, don't jump from the tall tree in the garden, don't eat and then swim, don't make big life choices without running them past the entire family. Don't be gay. I was used to my mom having an opinion on everything.

"Can we talk?" she asked.

"You might as well come out and say what you want to say, Mom. Then you can leave."

She started to cry again, and I was confused. I'd expected an argument, temper, pleading, anything but the silent tears. Maybe I should leave the room, let Mom have her meltdown all to herself.

But what if Mia wakes up and sees a crying grandmother, albeit one with a blurry face. What psychological damage could that do to her? Wait. I'm overthinking this. I sat next to Mom on the bed and tried to shake the negative feelings from me.

"Why are you here?"

She reached blindly for my hand and gripped it.

"This is all my fault. Do you remember the day you came home from school and told me you liked boys?"

"I do."

"It was a Friday, the third of May, two days after my

birthday, and we were going out for dinner that night to celebrate. It was raining, and there was lightning. Do you remember?"

Of course I did. Not the weather or the fact that we'd been going out for my mom's birthday. I did recall running home from school, convinced that I needed to talk to someone about the way I felt, about the epiphany I'd had in my math class, sitting behind Mikey Westman. I was gay, and I'd run straight to my mom, to the one woman who would tell me how things were and what I needed to do.

"I said, I remember."

"You told me that you wanted to kiss Mikey Westman and that you were gay."

"You don't need to summarize the entire messed up conversation."

I'd wanted her to tell me that she had my back, and that she loved me, and that it didn't matter. What I didn't want was a lecture about God, and Hell, and how me choosing to be gay was probably just a phase.

She shook her head and squeezed my hand so tight I thought she would cut off my circulation.

"I'm sorry I didn't hug you as hard as I could."

What? "Huh?"

She touched my arm. "When you told me how you felt, I don't think I said I loved you."

"You didn't say that, no." My chest hurt. "You told me I was wrong."

"I do love you, Ash."

"Are you sure?"

Her face fell.

"Ash, please, let me explain. A child should never have to earn a parent's love by being something they're not; a parent's love should be unconditional and forever. I let you down. I drove you away when I should have done the right thing. That was my job, but I messed it up."

"So what you're implying is that I'll do the same thing with Mia? Why? Because I'm gay or a single dad?" I stood up. "I think you should leave."

"No, this isn't about you. I didn't do the right thing. Me."

Silence. An awful loaded silence, where Mom stared at me, waiting for me to say something. What did I say?

"I want you to be happy," she finally said.

I was exasperated. "But I *am* happy, Mom. I don't see why you can't understand that."

"Little Mia is so perfect. I want her to be everything she can be, and that is all I wanted for you too." She shook her head, turned a tearful gaze to me. "But your dad… I ruined everything by trying to protect you, by sticking to God's rules."

"Don't start with your God," I warned.

She pressed a hand to her temple. "I didn't mean to. I'm at a different church now, not the one that kept me strong when your dad was alive and after. Not the one that told me that I could survive being married to an alcoholic if only I believed." She crumpled then. "The God that kept me sane drove you away, and I have no defense."

Okay, I could listen to this, give her a chance.

"What does your new church teach?"

"That I don't have to choose," she said, so simply that the words became more powerful. "It won't be easy being single and a father, Asher."

And now she starts again. "Mom—"

"I wish you'd found someone other than Darius to love so that there were two of you here."

She's not the only one. I waited for her to add that she wished I'd met a woman, but she didn't.

"One day I'll find someone, but right now, Mia is my priority."

"It's so hard doing it on your own," she said. "Your dad wasn't the kind of person I could rely on, and when I needed help, I turned to the church, and they became the support I didn't have. I was so black and white, but it was the only way I could protect myself. I know I sound crazy, but I've been seeing a therapist, and he's shown me the things I did that were inexplicably awful."

"Good," I said, then hurried to qualify that statement. "Good about the therapist I mean."

"He's gay you know, married, with three children, the oldest one is starting college in the fall."

"Oh."

"He showed me that I was questioning my place in your world, and losing control of you or your sister terrified me. Am I making any sense?"

All I knew was that the tightening of my chest had lessened a little. "Some."

"Don't question what role you have in Mia's life to the point where you tell her that any decisions she makes are wrong. Promise me."

"I promise." It was an easy vow to make. I wasn't

going to make Mia feel as if any of her options were the wrong ones.

We sat in silence for a moment. Then Mom sat upright and wiped her face furiously with tissues.

"I'm a silly old woman," she announced.

I wanted affection to flood me, something that had been missing for so long where our relationship was concerned, but I was still cold.

"Mom, you're only fifty-four," Siobhan said from the door. I glanced over at her, wondering how long she'd been standing there.

"I'm a grandmother now. I feel old because my time as your mom is coming to an end."

Siobhan huffed, "You'll always be our mom."

Luckily, Mia stirred in her crib and we both turned to stare back at the reason for all this emotion between us. Mom lost her thread, and I was glad for it.

"She's due a feed," I explained and checked my watch again.

Like clockwork, four hours had passed. The stirring increased, and Mia let out a small mewl of complaint, so I scooped her up and out of the crib, then went over to the changing table, dealing with the diaper as efficiently as I'd learned, and then with the tiny snaps on her sleeper shut, I picked her up and cradled her to my chest. Mom didn't mention the disposable diaper once and was crying again. I felt like joining her, but when something as simple as changing my baby's diaper became an emotional bonding moment, it was important one of us kept control of their feelings.

This was too much to process, and I didn't know

how I felt about any of it. Seeing my mom cry messed with my head.

We went downstairs, Siobhan made lunch, and then the six of us settled in the garden room, the doors open to the beautiful day. I ate one-handed, the other supporting the bottle as Mia lay tucked into my lap, drinking her formula. Debs and Evan were on the floor, and Siobhan was writing an email to Dan.

"Mia's so beautiful," Mom said again. "I think she has your coloring. Did the woman who donated the eggs… do you know her?"

We were doing this? We were talking about surrogacy?

"I don't know who donated the eggs, only that there was screening and the profile said she had brown hair and dark eyes the same as me. I wanted that so that Mia might look a little like me."

Mom vanished and then came back with her huge purse, pulling out an album packed full of baby photos of me and Siobhan that I remembered well.

"See?" She thrust the book under my nose to show me a classic shot of two tiny babies, one in blue, one in pink, and the two of them looked as if they were holding hands. "Mia looks the image of you and your sister when you were babies."

I examined the photo of us, and then down at Mia. "She does."

"You and Siobhan never wanted to be apart as babies, not from day one, but look at you now, living such independent lives. I'm so proud of both of you."

I waited for the *but*, the added part of how once I'd

decided to be gay I shouldn't have even thought of having a baby on my own. However, Mom closed the book and settled back on the sofa.

"Can I have a cuddle with my granddaughter?"

Nothing was really settled between us. I still felt an ache in me whenever I recalled some of the things she'd said in the past. But if I ever said anything to Mia that made her mad, I'd desperately hope that she forgave me. So maybe I should do the same. Not today, but one day?

"Of course."

She took Mia from me and cradled her close, glancing at me when I yawned widely.

"I remember when I was so tired I could fall asleep at the drop of a hat. We have Mia. You should get some rest, sweetheart."

"I'm not tired," I fibbed.

When I woke up, it was night time, and the only light was from the front room where a tiny fish tank sat in the corner. Seemed like it was just me and my rainbow fish down here, but after I managed to quell the instant panic, I followed the sound of voices, recognizing my mom's as one of them. When I rounded the corner, it wasn't my mom or Siobhan holding Mia. It was Sean holding my daughter, and I snapped. In a smooth move, I took Mia from him and stepped back.

"What do you want?" I asked as he moved in the opposite direction until his ass hit the work surface. One kissing session didn't mean he could waltz in when I wasn't there and hold Mia.

"I was just bringing over some food I made that I thought you might like, and then I met your mom. I have chili." He opened the pot, and the scent filled the air, and my stomach rumbled. "I made cornbread as well." He took the lid off a tray, and it smelled like heaven.

We were at an impasse. I'd flown into the kitchen all protective, snatching my daughter from his hold, acting like a crazy person, even though Siobhan had been there watching Mia. He, on the other hand, had brought me over dinner.

My mom shot me a curious glance, then inclined her head in that age-old gesture of *say something*.

"Thank you," I offered, but I wasn't going to apologize for acting like a mad man over the safety of my daughter. She was mine to protect, and it seemed as if no one else understood that single vital fact.

"I'm taking Mom and the kids out to eat," Siobhan said and herded Debs, Evan, and Mom to the door. Only when the front door shut did I realize they'd left me alone with Sean.

"They told me to tell you that Mia was just changed and your mom fed her," Sean reported, still plastered to the opposite side of the kitchen as if he thought I was going to charge him or something. I owed the man an apology, despite the fact that he was in my house uninvited.

"You brought food," I said instead or more like blurted.

He brightened and relaxed a little. "It's chili, but I

left out most of the chilies because I don't know how hot you'd like it." He touched a finger to his lip, "I just recall you put hot sauce on your burger that I tasted when we kissed, so I thought chili was a good bet."

"I love it hot," I announced, then felt heat in my face as if I'd admitted that fact about sex rather than a dinner of chili.

"I'll dish some up if you want to get settled somewhere." He waited.

"Okay, yeah, thank you." I still felt muddle-headed from sleeping and only wanted to go back to bed, but I distinctly remembered from childcare class back at the clinic that it was important to take help and support when it was offered, and I shouldn't mess up a neighborly donation of food.

I situated Mia in her little seat next to the breakfast table, then washed my hands, and at last there was nothing to do but sit down. There was only one bowl of chili and bread on the table, one set of silverware, and I was just about to ask him if he was eating as well when he beat me to it.

"Okay, that's me out of here," he announced and made a show of checking his watch. "I'm on shift in an hour, so I need to go." He crouched by Mia and placed his hand on her head before cupping her cheek and taking her hand. She was dozy, with eyes half-closed. "Bye, Mia, be good for your daddy, because he's very tired," he murmured. Then he turned his attention to me, his blue gaze piercing. "Can I kiss you?" he asked.

"Huh?" was the extent of my reply.

He chuckled and tilted my chin with a finger. Then

he kissed me as if he was never going to kiss me again, and I stood then wrapped my arms around him. I wanted this kiss. Hell, I wanted more than just a kiss, and for a few moments I forgot myself.

He gripped my ass, pulled me so close, and I swear I heard someone whimper. I suspected it was me. He slid his fingers past my waistband. The only thing holding me upright was one of his hands on my ass and the table itself. He deepened the kiss as he wrapped his fingers around my cock. I was so turned on, so damn hard, and part of me knew I should've been reciprocating, but all I could do was hold on for the ride. He crowded me against the table, and this time, I definitely let out a sound that was more growl than moan.

"You're so sexy," he said, then released his hold on me. I'd been so close to losing it. Why was he stopping? I opened my mouth to ask. Then he tugged me around the corner and out of sight of Mia, who was asleep anyway, and then in a smooth move, he went to his knees. He pulled down my sweats and boxers, hooking them under my balls, and there was no hesitation from him. Circling my cock with his fingers, he licked across the crown and hummed appreciatively. "Gorgeous," he murmured as he closed his lips around me and filled the remaining space with his hand.

"Fuck…" I know I tried to say more, but I couldn't, and I gave myself over to the sea of sensation that washed over me. I stared down, pulled my T-shirt out of the way, to see this gorgeous man with his lips around my cock, and the sight of him, the sensation of him sucking, the pressure on my balls from the material there, and I was gone.

"Sean," I warned, and he stopped sucking me, concentrating on slipping his hand up and down my length, and there was no coming back from this. He caught the come in his other hand, held me through the waves of the most perfect orgasm, and then he left me standing there. I heard running water, and then he was back, helping me to straighten my clothes before kissing me. He was still hard, and I reached for him, but he batted my hand away.

"Another time," he murmured, kissed me one last time, then with a casual wave, he left. I didn't let out the breath I'd been holding until I heard the front door shut behind him.

The chili was wonderful, not too hot, but spicy enough to wake me up, and Mia slept through the entire meal. I cleaned up a bit, washed up the pot for the chili and the bread container and resolved to return them tomorrow. I even answered a few emails, losing myself in re-planning deadlines. The only project I had outstanding was the final draft for a new car racing game that I was coordinating, and I could do that in my sleep.

I couldn't help laughing. I was doing everything asleep right now.

But I wouldn't have had it any other way.

Brady: Hey, you there?
Ash: Here, watching Game of Thrones from the

beginning. Only it's on mute so I don't wake Mia. You okay?

Brady: I could use a hug

Ash: {{{HUG}}} does that help?

Brady: :(Sometimes I just want a real hug, but then I realize that won't happen

Ash: I could visit

Brady: …

Brady: Maybe. One day, but not now

We hadn't talked much about why he was so convinced he would never meet someone to love. Also he was adamant he wasn't ready for us to meet in person. Both of those things made me sad, but I wasn't going to push him. He was someone I turned to when the nights were dark and I felt lonely, and we had a connection.

Brady: Night

Ash: {{{MORE HUGS}}}

Brady: ROFL. X

FIFTEEN

Sean

A combination of an accident on the freeway, a drive-by shooting, along with a suspected outbreak of measles, plus associated walk-ins had the ER in chaos. Not that chaos was bad. In fact, chaos in the ER was the norm, and it made time fly. It just had to be managed, and I didn't envy our attending, Noah, who stared at the board. I was standing with everyone else, waiting for the shootings and the vehicular pileup to arrive, scheduled for the same time, and we all checked with him for guidance.

"Can Mercy take any?" someone asked from my right.

Noah glanced at the source of the comment, a wet-behind-the-ears intern who was on his third day of his ER rotation. He looked so young, and even though he was just two years younger than me, it didn't matter. I still saw him as a kid. The glance Noah gave the intern spoke volumes, and the kid moved behind Reuben Gray, chief nurse and built like a brick outhouse, as Noah began dishing out his orders.

"… I want you at the door on triage, follow the first shooting that gets here, take two interns with you. I want tight, and I want fast, and let's get them stable and up to the OR if needed. Sean, RTA…"

I didn't wait for the rest, pointing at the three closest interns, as well as calling on the nurses we could spare, and gesturing for Reuben to follow.

"What have we got?" I asked him as we headed straight for the main intake doors.

"Jackknifed truck, driver dead, seven cars involved in the RTA, unknown victims, firefighters on site, ETA on V1, three minutes."

The rest passed in a blur. V1, or patient one, was a DOA. V2 on our table was a five-year-old kid with a head injury. The third was a man screaming for his wife. He appeared to have superficial wounds but collapsed, and we lost him on the table twice before stabilizing him after internal bleeding.

Miranda from Pastoral Care was a constant presence today. She supported the family of an elderly lady who'd passed in the ambulance bay long before we could get help to her. The woman had been eighty-three and even if she'd still been alive when we got to her she wouldn't have been a priority on the board, as she'd been picked up with symptoms of flu. Flu was trumped by a GSW or being the victim bleeding out after being cut from a car. We didn't have the staff, but how could we tell anyone that we had such horrific choices thrust upon us?

That was the terrible price we had to pay in the ER, the split-second judgments in life-and-death situations.

"We need to get this patient up to the OR. Also, we have another driver to clear and get to the cath lab. Cardiology is waiting," Noah said.

He was at my side, checking notes, his gaze taking in the unconscious father on the table, and he was talking at the same time. I was listening but staring at the monitor for the kid we'd pulled back from the brink. Until I could see that the patient was stable, he was going nowhere. In an instant, the rhythm changed, and I slammed the door open.

"Get him to the OR," I announced to the room, and there was a whirlwind of action, and Noah accompanied the victim up in the elevators to the OR.

When everything had been cleared, there was silence, and with it came what the worst part of everything. With the immediate urgency passed, all that was left was the debris of chaos, the blood painting the floors and tables, and the cleanup began. We still had another five hours left on shift, when the last of the wounded came in. All I could see was the uniform, the thick rubber boots, and the hand hanging from the side of the gurney. A firefighter, pushed in by paramedics who didn't seem in a big hurry.

Eric? Fuck? Was that Eric? Was the firefighter deceased? My heart stopped, and I lurched forward, still halfway between the fiery passion of taming chaos and the comedown of getting through it all.

I moved closer, seeing it was actually a young firefighter called Adam, the newest addition to Engine sixty-three. He was lying on the gurney, only because the paramedics were holding him there.

"I'm okay," he protested, even though blood dripped down his hand and onto the floor. I pushed my way through the accompanying firefighters who'd crowded around him, spotting Eric, so damned happy to see him standing upright. He looked right at me, and I saw the fear in his eyes, but I couldn't talk. I was listening to the paramedics with the stats I needed.

"Rebar is stuck between vertebrae…" I listened and assessed at the same time.

"We can stabilize him here, then get him upstairs." I patted Adam on the arm. "You're in safe hands," I said and marked the chart. This was a triage job, and people better than me would attempt to remove the rebar without paralyzing him, but I wasn't leaving his side.

Someone jostled and pushed past me, but I didn't get a chance to react before a woman with clothes burned from her side gripped hard on Adam's good arm.

"Thank you," she said, "Oh my God, I can't… my son is okay… you saved him. I owe you everything."

Adam coughed, and blood flecked his lips, but he nodded.

I held Adam's hand all the way to the OR. He didn't let go, but not once did he cry or make any other kind of sound.

"They can do good things here," I said as the doors shut between us, and he was wheeled away. He gave me a shaky thumbs-up, and my heart broke for him. Miracles were something we could indicate might happen for a patient, but we could never promise to make things right.

"Think he'll make it?" Eric asked from my side. I didn't even realize he'd followed us up, and I turned to look at him. He was exhausted, soot lined his face, and he was grim. "We tried to get him to stop. Damn fool wanted to be a hero. Climbed straight into the car, overpass wall collapsing around him, got the kid out, shielded him with his body."

"It's what you would do," I said, and he didn't argue. It's what we'd all do if it came to it. "The mom came over, thanked him for saving her son. I think Adam *was* a hero, don't you?"

"He should have waited," Eric murmured and leaned back against the nearest wall. "I could have gone in with him…"

"He acted on instinct, I guess? He did what he was trained to do."

Eric closed his eyes and nodded. "I know that." With a loud sigh, he pushed himself away from the wall that seemed to be the one thing holding him upright. "I'll be downstairs with the rest of the guys."

There was no point in me telling him to go back to the station or home or to get himself checked out. He was going to stand with the rest of the shift and wait for Adam to come around from surgery. I still had some time left on shift, but already felt like I'd run a marathon. I didn't hold out any hope that the rest of the night would be quiet, and it wasn't.

The bright light on the horizon was that Adam had made it through initial surgery; they'd managed to remove the rebar that was close to his vertebrae and next up was attempting to save his arm, but it was all about the waiting now to find out what would happen next for the kid.

I arrived home as dawn painted the sky with soft blues and pinks, and bypassed the house, grabbing a beer from the cooler in the garage and heading for the garden, Cap trailing behind me. Heading to the very farthest point from the house, past the pool, I then sat on one of the chairs we'd placed there with the views out over the valley, scratching Cap behind the ears and attempting to relax. I was alone for thirty minutes, and I hadn't even drunk any of the beer when Leo joined me.

"Bad night?"

"No worse than usual," I lied. Leo didn't have to know that for one awful moment I thought it had been Eric on the gurney.

Eric joined us, bringing his own beer, and together we stared out at a new San Diego morning in silence. Last night hadn't been anything different from what we saw nearly every day.

"How's Adam?" I asked.

"He has his family there," Eric said, which didn't answer the question at all. "Docs say he'll live." Unspoken was the extra, 'and that is all we can hope for'.

There'd been pain tonight; some who lived; others who died, and it was what the three of us dealt with the best way we could.

And the aftermath? Sitting nursing beers we wouldn't drink, toasting to the ones we lost or the ones we hoped would live. We would stay until one of us broke the silence again.

After last night? I knew it wouldn't be me.

Leo left at eleven for his shift, Eric had the rest of the day to himself, and after a shower and walking Cap, he went back to the hospital to check on Adam, who was now playing a waiting game. I was due back in the ER for the night shift, but the things that normally filled my day, sleeping, laundry, shopping, eating real food, everything paled next to the insistent need to see Ash. I could hang around in the garden or go and sit on the front porch, all in the hope I'd spot him, but today I felt it might be okay to knock on his door. Instead I called Cap for a walk, and he couldn't believe his luck that another of his favorite humans wanted to take him out. I sat him down and stroked behind his ears.

"Cap, I need you to look real cute when we go next door. Okay?"

Cap wagged his tail, then let out a low woof of agreement, which was probably more of a protest that I had put on his leash and then made him sit down. The woof was more of a "can we hurry up" than an "okay, I'll be cute" response. I ruffled his fur and headed next door.

"Hi," Ash said when he answered and checked behind me. I don't know what he was expecting, but I hoped it wasn't Eric or Leo, because this morning he only had me. "Is everything okay?"

I pasted on my best and most sincere smile and gestured at Cap on his leash. "I'm going for a walk, and I'd love coffee," I announced. "Do you and Mia want to come to the park?"

He frowned and looked at his watch, did that complicated math equation whereby he balanced baby sleeps with changes and food, while I waited. Then he brightened and gave me a smile.

"That would be great. Hang on." He gestured for me to step inside. "I just need to get Mia." As he went upstairs, I stayed where I was, right inside the front door, checking all the tiny differences between our house and his. Aside from the obvious one, there was evidence of Mia everywhere—a new pack of diapers at the base of the stairs, two piles of clean pink sleepers on the unit next to it, and the scent of the place was a combination of baby powder and Ash.

If I bottled this smell, I could be a millionaire. Then again, maybe it was me and my lust for Ash that was making me feel all kinds of turned just by seeing the man, let alone clocking the scent of him.

He came downstairs with Mia in his arms. She seemed to have changed in the hours since I'd last seen her. Her neck was stronger, she was holding her head away from Ash's chest, and I swear her eyes widened as I drew closer to kiss her head.

"I think she knows me," I said and held out my hands for her while Ash fixed up the stroller and packed enough bags to support army maneuvers.

"You're still a blur to her," he explained.

Of course I knew that, but the fanciful side of me

that kind of needed a baby to know me decided to ignore empirical evidence.

"Whatever. She knows her Uncle Sean, don't you, sweetheart." I tickled under her chin, then broke into an impromptu swaying dance with her around the hall, only stopping when it was obvious that Ash was staring at me with amusement on his face. "What can I say? I like babies."

The memory of last night, of the young boy that Adam had saved, and how the other surgeons had nearly lost Adam flashed through my thoughts, but I forced it back. Unless I could compartmentalize everything I saw, then how could I even think of forming an attachment to a little soul like Mia?

We headed out to the park, taking the shortcut to the back and then walking the perimeter.

"Can I ask you something?" Ash asked as we passed the swings.

I was in the middle of untangling Cap's leash from where he'd gone around a tree the wrong way from me, and I smiled at Ash. "Of course."

"I saw Eric this morning. He came over to say hello to us, but I think it was Mia he really wanted to see."

"Yeah?"

"I thought something might be wrong, and the news this morning was all about the pileup on the freeway. I assume he answered the call?" I nodded, and he sighed. "They said they took the injured to Soledad Memorial. I guess… was that you dealing with it all?"

"Some of it." I downplayed what had happened because a civilian didn't need to know what kinds of things we saw or hear about the people we'd lost. He stopped walking then, and I didn't realize until I was a couple of steps ahead of him. I turned to see what was wrong, and he was staring right at me.

"They showed a family being pulled from a car, a child."

Shit. This was all of a sudden going to be a hundred kinds of awkward. If he thought for one minute that Eric and I had wanted to see Mia, just to make things balance in our heads, then he'd freak.

"Yeah," I said, remaining cautious.

"Did the boy… was he okay?"

"He was fine, a few scratches, and his mom came away unhurt. The dad is still in ICU, but he'll pull through." I put a positive spin on what had been some impossibly awful details.

"What about the firefighter who was trapped?" Ash bit his lip. "I thought maybe… I was worried when I heard and they didn't release a name, that it was Eric."

"Adam. The firefighter is called Adam. He'll be okay." *I hope.*

"I know you can't talk about it…" He lifted Mia from the stroller and stepped closer to me, taking my hand and lacing our fingers on Mia's head. "But I get why Eric needed to see Mia, and now you can see her as well."

The compassion in his voice undid me, and emotion choked me as I returned his steady gaze over Mia's head. He wasn't running for the hills or pulling back from us in terror at what we might tell him. Instead he understood how we might need proof of life, and that was a precious gift to give Eric, and me.

Only he didn't fully understand what *I* needed.

"It wasn't just Mia I wanted to be with," I said, and I dropped the leash and stood on it. Then with my free hand, I cupped his face. We were hidden here behind the trees that ringed the park, alone and safe, and all I wanted to do was kiss him.

"Really?" he murmured and met me halfway, his head tilted until we fit perfectly. The kiss was everything I felt inside me, the action from last night, the pain I'd seen in Eric's face, the stoic heroism in Adam as he lay in agony, the joy in the mother collecting her son, warring with the pain of waiting to see if her husband would live. There was lust and need all wrapped up in this kiss, and when we separated, Ash rested his forehead on mine.

"You're not supposed to be happening to me," he said. When he moved back a little way and looked at me steadily, it was as if something passed between us. Maybe a recognition of what was happening between us, a flicker of something that was more than just lust. Something profound and as necessary as my next breath. "It was supposed to be just me and Mia," he said, "but I don't want to…"

He didn't finish, and instead he kissed me again before moving right out of my reach. He was distancing himself in this public place, but he had a soft smile curving his lips.

"Coffee?" I suggested and picked up the leash again, scratching Cap's fur and praising him for being patient.

"And cake?" Ash asked with a widening smile.

By the time we sat down with coffee and cake, the emotional kiss and compassion had been filed away, and we talked sports, weather, and even touched on politics before we decided that was way too depressing.

On the way back, we stole more kisses, and the whole situation was surreal.

When I yawned, he told me to get some sleep, but there was one thing I needed to make him promise first.

"My next night off, I want to make you dinner and bring it to your place, so we can look out for Mia."

"Okay—"

"On a date," I interrupted, just to be clear about what I was asking.

He dimpled a smile and nodded.

I backed away then, nearly tripping over a dozing Cap, and tumbling down the steps off his porch to end up looking like an idiot, but his smile didn't waver.

"Bye." I left then because otherwise, I'd have been on his porch all day, and I really needed sleep.

SIXTEEN

Asher

Would you like to meet up?

The words at the end of the email hung there. The guy in charge of the support forum, Nick, sent me a private email to suggest that I meet with their small group of single dads this weekend. I didn't have an excuse. I wasn't busy. There were no planned visits from family. I wasn't ill. Mia wasn't ill. In fact I didn't know what stopped me from saying yes straight away.

I approached most problems in life in a similar way to game design. I would create a critical path analysis in my head, working out all the interdependent details, and somehow using that process, I was managing my life okay. I was confident, owned my own company, and the only thing that had ever pushed me off track was my momentary madness and need to believe that Darius was good for me.

So I looked at the reasons why I wasn't writing an instant reply and analyzed my thought process.

Nick was a bereaved dad of three, with two boys, brothers, aged eight and ten to move on, of needing to put his children first. Actually, he appeared put together and in charge of his life. He'd adopted both boys when they were little, but his daughter had been born through surrogacy, the same as Mia. He'd been there, done that, and got a million best-dad T-shirts, I was sure of that fact. His daughter was an avid dancer, his boys both played baseball, and they'd vacationed last year in Orlando. I knew all this because his Instagram was full of photos of his family.

Of course he was grieving; his husband had lost the battle with cancer, and I couldn't for one minute think what that must have been like for the husband, for Nick or for their kids. Yet he was still running this support group, and he had all this experience, and then there was me.

I felt I was doing okay, more than okay. I felt more awake and in control, and I wasn't messing up diapers anymore, although I still struggled to handle the really messy ones because I didn't think the advice out there would be for me to take Mia in the shower with me to wash her off. I didn't shave every day, and I was weeks past a decent haircut, but I dressed every day, and I showered, so to me, that was a win.

Ash: *Are you there?*
 Brady: *On my phone.*
 Ash: *The San Diego forum members have a meetup planned.*

Brady: *I heard it's a good group, you should go.*

Ash: *I don't know if I'm ready?*

Brady: *Don't be like me and stay inside alone. You are ready.*

Ash: *Will you come with me?*

Brady: ...

Brady: ...

Brady: *I can't. Not yet. It's still too much.*

I never asked him what he meant, and he never told me, but something was going on with him that meant he didn't want to interact with other people. Or maybe it was just the group, or even just me. I got the feeling that if I ever really asked that it might scare him off forever and I didn't want that.

When Brady signed off, I started writing an email, rocking Mia gently on my shoulder where she dozed, trusting that her dad was there for her.

"Okay, Mia, this is easy. Just send an email back saying you'll go, and maybe explain how you're nervous and have reservations."

It was all about not having been out in public, and how I felt that people would judge me as a dad on my own, as a gay man who chose to have a child, about surrogacy, about the fact that I haven't shaved in three days. Everything went down. All my insecurities spilled out of me in one long letter filled with adjectives. It wasn't to send; it was just me getting all my insecurities out.

Then I backspaced and deleted it all.

I began again, detailing how it was difficult for me to get there. Which was a lie.

"Delete, delete, delete, for fuc—fudge sake. Sorry, Mia."

So now what? I wasn't doing anything on Saturday. What if the best thing right now was to meet up with this group and talk face-to-face? Brady said I should go, and this Nick guy wasn't going to laugh at me or judge me, I was letting my own insecurities color my expectations of what I would find there.

Hi Nick, I'll be there, thank you. I signed it *Ash*, and wrote *Ash Haynes* under just in case, and that was it. I'd committed to meeting this whole new world of people. I copied in Brady in the hope that he would see it and come as well. I could meet him face-to-face, something we'd been working our way toward, although he seemed reluctant. Something about the pressures of family life and work. Mostly I think that he'd been Lucas and Maddie's dad for so long now that he'd forgotten how to connect with other people. Although when we chatted, I noticed he very carefully avoided talk of friends or his past.

Gently cradling Mia, I made my way up to my bedroom and placed her in the crib, tucking her in and watching the rise and fall of her chest. My love for her was overwhelming, and my heart ached with it.

"Love you, Mia," I murmured and then lay back on my mattress, turning on my side so I could watch her sleep. She was beautiful, her skin so soft. Her downy hair looked a little thicker now, but not by much. I wonder what color it will be and if she would care that it was her dad who would braid it for school.

I closed my eyes and imagined the complicated plait that I'd often watched Siobhan do. "I'll ask your aunty Siobhan about braiding your hair, Mia, and it will be the best hair in school," I murmured and then fell asleep.

Siobhan and Mom surprise-visited just past three in the afternoon and woke me up. Before Mia, I'd never have thought of sleeping in the middle of the day, but I felt recharged enough that I allowed Siobhan to hustle me into the bathroom.

"What are you doing here?" I demanded.

"Debs is at a sleepover with friends, Evan is at soccer camp, and we wanted to see you and Mia."

"What?"

"Well, Mom doesn't want to miss out."

"You mean as she's missed out on most of my life." Sue me if I still had a bitterness inside me that was taking a while to subside.

"Stop it, Ash, and shave," she ordered. "You look like a hobo."

"Thanks, sis." I sighed and then watched as Siobhan took Mia to change her and fuss over her. I assumed Mom was downstairs, but knowing she was there didn't make me quite as tense as it might have done, not with Siobhan being down with her. Maybe one day I could have Mom in the house and not go on the defensive, but today wasn't that day. The shave was amazing, the shower was bliss, and I let myself enjoy every second of it. Today was the first day I felt like a normal human being, and my thoughts wandered in the shower to Sean and the kisses in the park and the blow job in the kitchen. He'd kissed me so thoroughly on every occasion that I could still taste him now.

Memories of his clever mouth, with the sucking, and the kisses, and his tongue licking mine, tangling with it, running the length of my cock, made me hard. With the hot water beating down on my shoulders, I circled my cock to thoughts of him sucking me and got myself off in the quickest time ever.

As I dried my hair with the towel I couldn't help but wonder if there would be more blow jobs. Or would we skip that and go straight for the big stuff? I wasn't averse to that idea, but part of me also thought it would be nice to have some grown-up conversation alongside orgasms.

When I arrived in the kitchen, still buttoning my shirt, Mom was cleaning work surfaces with a concerted scrubbing action that spoke of experience, Siobhan was rocking Mia and eating a cookie, and everything was calm.

"You look almost human." Siobhan smirked.

"Ha-ha." I stole the cookie from her hand and ate it in one mouthful, doing my best hamster impression. "Afternoon, Mom," I said, although it sounded more like an mmph-flmph as crumbs flew everywhere. Seeing my mom in my house caused me to have the strangest reaction. I guessed it was shock, but I assumed that in the end, I would feel okay with it, and resolved to follow Siobhan's insistence I give Mom a chance. Only, what if things changed? What if I trusted her and she turned on me again?

I still felt resentment in the pit of my stomach, and I couldn't fight it most of the time. I had to come to terms with the echoes of past hurts. Mom glanced up from her cleaning, and her smile was cautious. I wanted to be able to hug her and reassure her because my thoughts were sharper, and I wondered if it was time for me to understand and forgive. Mia deserved to have her grandmother in her life. I wish I knew how I felt for real, but the only things I was certain about now were Mia, Siobhan, and my career.

Don't forget Sean. You want to spend time with him, kiss him, maybe do way more with him.

Mom poured three coffees, and we took them out to the garden and sat in the shade. My house was elevated compared to next door, and I could see over the fence to the pool beyond. Who knew where this thing with Sean would lead? It might be all fireworks that flamed bright and then died in an instant. And wouldn't that make us being neighbors a hundred kinds of uncomfortable?

Do I want sex that bad that I will maybe fuck everything up for us being harmonious neighbors?

"… so I said it was none of her freaking business and that she was a miserable old bat and that my son could do whatever the hell he wanted to do."

"Huh?" I caught the tail end of whatever my mom had been getting worked up about. "What?"

"Sheila, you know, from my book club, going on about a child with two dads was bad enough, but you bringing a child into the world as a single father…" She waved her hand dramatically. "I stood up and gave an impassioned speech, and that put her in her place. Of course I've had to leave the book club."

Siobhan gasped. "They threw you out? They can't do that!"

"No, sweetheart." Mom patted her leg. "I resigned as co-chair and left. They were all as bad as each other, bunch of middle-class wannabes with superiority complexes. They never approved of me having a gay son, and kept saying I must be a bad parent." She glanced at me then, and there was that vulnerability in her eyes that made me feel like the bad guy. It seemed to me that her expression was one big question, and she was looking for reassurance that she hadn't somehow *made* me gay with bad parenting skills. Yet again we had that barrier between us, and I couldn't help the resentment returning. So much for finding peace. I could leave it, not challenge Mom's cautious words, but I had Mia to think of, and I was sick of the innuendo.

"No one chooses to be gay or is forced to be gay because of parenting." I was forceful, and I could see the minute Mom realized what she'd said, as she subsided miserably into the chair.

"I'm sorry. I didn't mean anything by that." She held her coffee close to her chest, and I felt like the biggest fucked-up son on the planet. How could we ever move past everything if I didn't take her word at face value that she was trying to be a better mom? I bet there would be a thousand times I'd mess up with Mia, and what would I want her to do if I did?

Forgive me. Understand I was from a different generation. Love me anyway.

"I know you say that, Mom. I'm still tired, and I still have all these old hurts." I reached out and held her hand. "I'm trying."

She teared up then, but I was done with seeing her cry. She needed to laugh, and we had to connect in happier times.

"What did the book club say about you leaving?"

She took my olive branch and ran with it.

"They said they didn't care, but then, you know what they don't realize? In the newsletter that I still sent, you'll never guess what book is up for them to read next?"

I had to play along because I could see some kind of punch line coming. "What?"

"*Call Me by Your Name.*" She snorted a very un-mom-like laugh. Then Siobhan joined in, and finally the irony hit me as well, and I joined in the laughter. My laughter woke Mia, and I took her from Siobhan, adjusting her hat to shade her eyes.

"Hi," Leo interrupted my thoughts as he called from over the fence, and he had to be standing on something to be able to see over, and I imagined him leaping the fence as Sean had in front of Siobhan.

I can't believe I missed Sean vaulting a fence. How goddamn sexy would that have been? Maybe I could get him to give me a private vaulting experience.

"Hello, young man," Mom said, and I sunk into my seat.

Surely, Leo would balk at being called that. Instead,

he grinned even wider. "Ma'am," he said and tipped an imaginary hat.

"Does he think he's a cowboy?" Siobhan said under her breath.

"Call me Barbara. This is my daughter Siobhan, and you probably know my son, Asher."

"Ash," I corrected.

Leo crossed his arms on the top of the fence and leaned there. "I've already met our new baby daddy," he observed. I hated that term because to me, it implied I only had Mia to help out a baby mommy. But there weren't a lot of things I could do that would change how the world labeled me now and would forever label me.

Not just Dad, but Gay Dad, which needed some kind of trademark.

Mia wouldn't have a dad. She would have the Gay Dad, but I was cool with that. I was going to raise a tolerant, understanding, beautiful child on my own, and I was going to look into the copyright for the title. So Leo was only teasing, but I kind of wished he wouldn't when my mom was right there.

Do you know how much having a dad who is gay will shape your child? The words she'd shouted at me when I told her what I was doing were front and center. The meaning behind them seemed laced with poison.

And there it was again, the resentment at her brutal assessment of what I'd planned to do. My chest tightened, and not even Leo's smiling and joking were breaking through the hard shell I was erecting around me.

Then Sean joined him at the fence, and my stupid heart skipped a beat.

"Is this man bothering you?" Sean deadpanned, "or do I need to call the cops?"

Sean abruptly disappeared from view in a mess of flailing arms as Leo shoved him, and for a second I sat upright in my chair, only relaxing when Sean popped back up like a jack-in-the-box.

"Mrs. Haynes, Siobhan," he said with a small wave, clearly none the worse for falling off whatever they were standing on.

Sean was a sight for sore eyes in his scarlet T-shirt, his arms crossed on the fence, and a broad smile splitting his face.

Leo stepped sideways and winced. "What?" he demanded, which made me think Sean had kicked him.

"Ask them," he prompted.

"Well, you might as well ask them."

"You said you would."

It was like watching Laurel and Hardy, and somehow the tension in me uncoiled until I realized I was smiling.

"So we're hoping to have a block party for the end of summer. You're all welcome, but we don't have a date yet, because it all depends on whether our shifts line up."

"You don't need to go into so much detail, dude," Leo faux-whispered.

"We'd love to," Mom said, and Siobhan echoed the sentiment.

Mia stirred on my lap and screwed up her face, all the warning signs for an imminent diaper change, and I stood up to take her inside. "Sorry, diaper change," I explained.

Sean stood upright. Then in a smooth move, he vaulted the fence between our properties landed like a superhero on my side. He even did that whole pause thing bent in a crouch before standing up and brushing himself down.

That is the sexiest thing I've ever seen.

"I'll help," he announced "meet you inside." Then he sauntered into my house as if he owned the place.

Siobhan stood and side-hugged me. "We have to make a move, I want to miss the traffic back home. You gonna be okay, little brother?" She kissed Mia's head and held out a hand to help Mom up. More kisses for Mia, a cautious hug for me from Mom, which I returned with disproportionate enthusiasm.

"I'm going to be good," I said, and for the first time I wasn't lying.

I waved them away, then headed inside. By now the diaper needed changing, but it was Sean who took Mia off me and carried her upstairs to the changing table, and it was him that changed Mia and spent a long time fussing her, kissing each of her toes, and humming as he worked.

"You feeling better now, princess?" he murmured and picked her up, patting her butt before turning to face me. His smile dropped, and it hit me I was staring at him like an idiot. "I'm sorry. I didn't mean to intrude—"

I cut off his words with a side-on kiss. "Do you know how hot that was? Vaulting the fence, then changing a diaper?"

He returned the kiss, but it was kind of awkward with Mia between us, and when she squawked at the delay in food, I took her from him and went downstairs to make a bottle. Heading to the sun-room, I then made us comfortable and listened as Sean cleared away mugs and plates into the dishwasher. For a few seconds, I could sit there and fantasize about what it would be like to have Sean in the house on a permanent basis, puttering around, sharing chores and my bed.

In fact, the complete opposite of being single.

"Is there anything I can do for you?" He set coffee on the small table at my side, then sat opposite me.

"You don't have to be here helping me. If you have time off, shouldn't you be sleeping?"

"Coming off nights, so I'm not back until eight in the morning, and I need to stay awake, try to get my routine back. Spending time with you and Mia is much more fun than sleeping." He bent forward and rested his elbows on his knees, his fingers laced together. "You'll come to the block party? You and Mia? And your family?"

"Mia and I definitely. I'm back working after this week, but I can fit in a day of fun."

"The date will depend on shifts, and we might not be able to give much notice."

That was an easy thing. "I work from home," I explained.

"Are you getting a nanny?"

"No, jeez, it's all on me. I need to get into a routine of working between feeds and sleeps, but it was always going to be me at home with Mia. Darius had been the one with the need to travel. What I do can be done from home mostly, and I've made good money, enough to own the house and not have to worry about working for a while." *Fuck, I sound so defensive.*

"What is it that your ex does?"

"Marine biologist, worked out of San Diego when we first met, then London. Now he's in Bali, or at least he was last I heard." I didn't mention he would be back in New York at some point in the future or that he wanted me to find a babysitter and fly all the way to the East coast as if it was nothing. He was over there. I didn't know when, and I didn't care. I was done with him, and I had Mia to think of and Sean sitting there all sexy *after* he'd just changed my daughter's diaper.

When I thought of all those shallow years where all I'd looked for in a man was a tight ass and pecs, Sean was the complete opposite. Not that he didn't have a tight ass or lacked pecs, but he was *real*, he had substance, and he was dangerous to my heart. I had to put Mia first in everything. No, that's wrong, I *wanted* to put Mia first.

"So tell me more about what you do?" Sean asked and looked so damned earnest, as if my answer to this was the most important thing he was going to hear ever.

"Do you play video games?"

Sean sighed. "Not really. Spare time is me sleeping."

"Well, that is what I do. I design characters."

"Do you draw them?"

"No. I code the information that makes the drawings work, but I can sketch enough to get me by."

"That's impressive. I can't even draw a stick figure. When I play Pictionary, I just stab at the stick man I always draw, as if that will help. Leo and Eric refuse to play with me, but then I refuse to play cards with them because they both cheat."

I looked down at Mia, who was dozing off, with her bottle nearly finished. No one had told me how much a baby sleeps. Of course, I knew that sleep was a thing that babies did and that yes, I should sleep when she did, but it was clear to me that she was the most perfect baby in the entire world. Feeding, sleeping, pooping, my baby girl was the best at it all. Now if only I could work myself around to being the best dad, then everything would be good.

I yawned widely, and Sean stood. I wanted to tell him not to go, that I was fine and I wasn't tired at all, but it was six now, and I knew Mia would be up at ten, and two, and then six in the morning, and I should make the effort to top off the sleep tanks.

Sean appeared to have a different idea. He led me upstairs, waited for me to put Mia in her crib, and then kissed me to the bed. We tumbled back on it, and he rolled onto his back and pulled me close, closing his arms around me and holding me tight.

"We both need sleep."

At first, I was confused, but he settled back on the pillow, pressed a kiss to the top of my head, and held me.

And in that very moment the protection around my heart cracked enough that I knew he'd get inside. This man was dangerous.

SEVENTEEN

Sean

When I was first home with my single beer, sitting on the edge of the pool with my feet in the water and my skin slippery from sunblock, I heard Mia crying and the soothing baritone of Ash singing nursery rhymes. The crying stopped, but the singing continued, carried to me on the breeze, and I felt all kinds of warm and fuzzy.

I had a date tonight with Ash, and anticipation was everything.

All I was waiting for was a text from Ash telling me Mia was fed and sleeping, and then I was taking over the beef stew I'd made, along with a basket of cornbread. It was simple food, but possibly the second tastiest thing I make after chili. I wanted to be over there now, helping with Mia, but he'd explained that he wanted things to be chilled when I got there.

Was it wrong to want to spend time, just the three of us, doing normal stuff like bath and bedtime?

"Good shift?" Leo interrupted my thoughts as he sat

next to me, Cap heading straight for the shade of the bushes.

Gun violence, vehicular chaos, cops and firemen milling around, a patient knocking our newest med student out cold.

"Meh, I'd give it a five."

"A quiet day."

"Always."

We toasted each other with beer, sat for a few moments longer.

"So you and Ash, then?" he asked.

"Yeah, me and Ash."

"He's a good guy. We like him. He's doing well with Mia."

I guess it was only me who could see the cracks in Ash, the worries and insecurities. Was that a good thing? Or a bad thing?

Nothing bad was slipping into my thoughts right now. Hell, everything was sunshine. The detritus of Leo's attempt at dinner was strewn across the kitchen, and it was fine. The fact that Leo had left his washing in the machine again, fine. That the remote control for the television had vanished altogether? That didn't matter at all.

I have it bad. Even worse after holding Ash in bed. At first, I'd wanted to do more, I wanted to kiss him everywhere and maybe hold him down and carry him over the edge again. The expression on his face when I'd been sucking him had been exquisite.

When I'd woken at eight to the vibration of my watch alarm, I hadn't wanted to leave Ash and had left a note where he would see it when he woke. I'd explained I was on the schedule at work, for the next day at least, knowing full well that my original twelve-hour shift was likely to extend way past that as it always did, but that if he was okay with it, I wanted to bring dinner to him on Friday. I asked him to text me if that wasn't okay, and even though I checked frequently, there'd been no text to say no. I only realized after the tenth time of checking that I should have done it the other way around. Then we could have exchanged texts in what had been a long shift with crazy peaks of frenetic activity. The first text I'd gotten from him, an hour ago, said that Mia had woken up, and could we delay starting. My chest tightened at the instinctive reaction that Ash was canceling, but once I read what he sent, I texted back my most nonchalant *cool* with added smiley emoji.

"Is that stew for all of us?" Leo asked as he followed me into the house.

"No. Take your wet clothes out of the machine."

Leo peered into the washer and cursed, lifting the items out and putting them straight into the drier.

"There, done. Now can I have some stew?"

"No, it's not for you and Eric. This is an Ash and Sean stew."

Leo snorted at that and made a dive, which I'd anticipated, straight for the oven. He tripped over my foot and ended up on the floor, laughing like an idiot and Cap standing with a paw on his chest.

"Why is the television remote wedged under the refrigerator?" he asked and eased himself out from under

Cap, who just wanted to play, then rolled over to extricate it.

"Your guess is as good as mine. Probably got kicked under there."

The front door slammed open, and Eric, fresh from shift, stalked in, muttered hello, grabbed a bottle of water from the fridge and some Tylenol, patted Cap, stepped over Leo, and headed into the hall before turning one-eighty and heading back in.

"What the hell are you doing on the floor?" he asked.

Leo rested back on his elbows. "I thought it was obvious. I was hiding the remote under the refrigerator so you couldn't watch any more *Mountain Men* episodes. Only Sean caught me hiding it and punched me out."

Eric blinked at Leo and then shook his head. "Children," he muttered and left the kitchen.

I held out a hand to help Leo stand, and at the same time, my phone vibrated with a text.

"Ready now." Leo reached it before me and read it out loud. "Looks like sexy neighbor is waiting for you." He waggled his eyebrows, and I kind of wanted to punch the idiot for real. I didn't have time for him. I put on oven gloves and lifted out the stew. The cornbread was already packed up and in the bag on my back, and within a minute of the text, I was heading next door.

"Don't do anything I wouldn't do," Leo said, his tone dripping with innuendo.

So what if I had lube and condoms in the same backpack as the cornbread? That was no one's business but mine and Ash's. I ignored him and walked right through the open door of Ash's house, Ash standing just inside, sexy and nervous all at the same time.

"That smells good," he said and closed the front door behind us, ushering me into the kitchen. He'd laid the silverware and plates on the table, and if I wasn't mistaken, there was soft music playing from the living room.

"Where's Mia?" I asked as I placed the stew on a cutting board to save the surface. I shrugged the bag off and dropped it onto the nearest chair.

"In her crib." He shook the receiver for the monitor. "I can hear her on this, but I need to check on her. I'm not sure I will ever stop worrying about her. Sorry."

I couldn't stop myself from kissing away the worry, and then the kissing became more, and dinner was forgotten. I don't know who moved first. I think we were both as desperate for more, but it was Ash who tried to tug me out of the kitchen.

"Are we doing this?" he asked, breathless, "I don't remember how to do sex."

"You'll remember quick enough—"

He shoved at me. "No, Darius said I wasn't very good in bed and I need to warn you—"

"Darius is an asshole—"

"But—"

"Shhh." Right now, I was focused on one thing and one thing only. "When you kiss me I self-combust, believe me when I say I'm going to come in my pants if we don't hurry up."

"Really?"

"Yeah, really. We need this." I pulled out the first thing in the backpack and held it up.

"Cornbread?" Ash said, confused. "Uhm?"

I glanced from him to what I was holding, and embarrassed I dug deeper and held up the condoms and lube. "Tada!"

Ash huffed a laugh. "I have a supply after today's visit to the pharmacy. I have it all, diapers, wipes, two new pacifiers, condoms, and lube." He hooked a finger into my belt loop. "I have everything, upstairs, ready."

I couldn't help myself. I buried my fingers in his hair and gripped hard, exposing his throat and kissing there, tasting every inch of skin I could find. He was doing the same back as we stumbled and kissed our way up the stairs. At one point, we almost fell right back down again, but he caught me, and laughing, we stopped at the top.

"I can't… not in there… are we okay to…?" He sounded so unsure, and after I got over the instant disappointment when he began with "I can't," I hugged him close.

"We don't have to do anything," I began, but he pressed a hand to my mouth.

"I just meant, Mia is in there, and I don't want to… not in that room…" Instead, he tugged me into another bedroom, the mirror of my room next door, and in one corner of the immaculate room was a single bed. Next to it was a small cabinet, and he wasn't joking when he said he'd bought supplies for any event. He grabbed a handful of whatever was there, and then turned to face me, holding it all my way.

I took everything he gave me and tossed it onto the mattress, then stalked him, kissing him down until we were both on the bed.

The *small* bed.

"Maybe the floor would be better?" I mused, but he wasn't letting me move, gripping my ass with one hand and yanking me down by my hair with the other. He was demanding and bossy, and I loved every second of it. He was in charge of the kiss, and I was just along for the ride, and fuck, but the kisses were hot. He possessed me. He took everything he needed, and when both of his hands were on my ass, he pulled me down against him, and we were both hard. I had never been kissed and wanted as much as this minute right here. I wanted to move on to skin, but at the same time, I didn't want to stop this delicious feeling of being on the edge of something magical. Anticipation was an aphrodisiac, and it was sending me wild.

"Fuck, the way you kiss."

He frowned, "I'm sorry if I'm too…"

"Give me more," I said as he slipped his hands up and under my shirt, smoothing them over my back, scratching the skin, and he broke the kiss, but only enough to push me up so he could get to the buttons of my shirt. I don't know what kind of shit Darius had thrown at him, but if I ever met the man I'd be explaining a few things about how hot Ash was.

I needed to get more involved and swatted his hands away, scrambling off him and stripping the quickest way I knew how. I wasn't watching him, but in my peripheral vision, I saw his clothes being discarded with just as much speed. He went to his knees on the bed, and I stepped into his arms, and we kissed some more. This time I could feel the warmth of his skin, the gentle touch of the hair on his chest as it rubbed my nipples, the sensation of cool air washing over us. Every one of my nerve endings was on fire, and I reached between us and circled his cock. He groaned into the kiss and bucked up into my gentle hold.

"I need this," he moaned and threaded his hands into my hair again. He loved to hold on. He clearly wanted to be active in us making love, and I wanted more than to have him writhing under me. The bed size was awkward. No way could two grown men get anything like purchase on it, and with a growl of frustration, I tugged him off the bed, and we stood and kissed.

"We have to get a bigger bed in here," I said, and for a second the kisses faltered, and he stepped back, his eyes widening. Was he scared of the thought that I wanted more than this? Did he not feel the same as I did? I had to ask him, but then he smiled.

"I'll order one tomorrow."

I kissed him then. I led the embrace. It was me telling him what to do, where to move, how to stand, and then I got all kinds of inspired.

"Turn around," I demanded, and he tripped over his jeans as he did what I'd told him, but I righted him before he fell ass over tail. With my front to his back, I nudged him to lean on the bed. Then I used my knee to widen his legs. After that I stood back and admired my new lover. He looked back at me, and his tongue darted out to wet his lips.

"Get a move on," he demanded, and I wasn't going to argue. I suited up, then after slicking my fingers, I stretched him before kissing him awkwardly. He jacked himself, and I reached around with my free hand to pull and twist his nipples. He moaned into the kiss, and I pushed on his back until he was bent over the bed.

"You're so fucking sexy like this," I muttered, smoothing my fingers over his balls, and he rocked, and I had to grip his hip to stop him. "Don't move... fuck..." On *my* timetable, I pressed inside, let his body accept me, waited, and then finally I was there, and I stopped, reaching for his cock and knocking his hand away.

He groaned but complied, and I pulled my cock out a little, waiting, then rocking back in.

"Fuck," he said on a breath.

My thighs burned with this position, but every thrust into the tightness made my head spin, and I ignored the burn. I twisted my hand, jacked him in time to my moves, and thank God he was so vocal. I knew what he was feeling. Every. Single. Movement.

"More," he pleaded. "Harder," he demanded.

I angled my body, and he covered my hands with both of his, his breathing harsh. Only when he was really close did I release my hold on him.

"Get yourself off," I ordered, and *fuck,* he did exactly what I'd said.

Forcing himself back on me, then forward into his hand. He was getting close. He told me so, and I was so close myself I had to let go. With a final thrust, I was rigid inside him, waves of orgasm taking every one of my breaths. He shouted his release and leaned back in my hold, twisting his neck for kisses, demanding we kiss as he came. When I was soft enough to pull out, after I'd wiped at his hands with my shirt, I tugged him to me, then fell back on the narrow bed, pulling him down, and we lay there, sticky and hot and completely sated.

"I've never…" he began.

I just held on tight. "Me neither."

EIGHTEEN

Asher

I took delivery of the double bed within forty-eight hours of Sean leaving. It wasn't anything fancy, but it was solid with a firm mattress, and there was plenty of room to spread out if we needed to.

If I want to.

He'd been at work nonstop since the hottest experience of my entire damn life. So there was no chance of a repeat of what had gone down on the smaller bed. That didn't stop me getting myself off to thoughts of what he'd done, and I was kind of sore, so I was reminded. What I wanted right now was more of his incendiary kisses, and I wanted him to hold me down and fight me for control. Of course I'd give in, but God, I really wanted him bad.

Then I wanted to talk to him as well. We'd talked, crammed together on the tiny bed, and he had all these stories about work. Not confidential stuff, but tales of midnight wheelchair races or betting on who had the most of a certain ailment in one night. He was interesting, funny, and he wanted to know about the things I did.

That was a new one. What I hadn't know about Darius' career wasn't worth mentioning, because he never shut up about it. But he'd never listened to me, never gave my career any attention.

And why was I even thinking about Darius? Not only was I comparing him to Sean and finding him lacking, but I'd had two texts from him. One last night after Sean had left, which said, *I'm in New York. Are you coming to see me?* I answered by sending him a simple *no*. I was happy here with my new life, a daughter who I would die for, who owned my heart, and a man who was not just on fire in bed but was funny and interested in *me*. So yeah, my *no* might have been harsh, but he hadn't sent me a whole string of emoticons or an x for a kiss. Not that I'd expected him to, and God knew how I'd handle it if he did. I'd have to call 911 to tell them he was suffering from brain trauma or something. In fact, no was a perfect and reasonable answer; I didn't owe him anything.

The other text had come in this morning. The message itself made no sense, and I could picture him as he wrote it, drunk, and probably on his own with his right hand for company. In summary, he wanted me, he needed me, and why wasn't he enough for me? Why had I ruined everything by wanting a child after he'd changed his mind?

I deleted the text and blocked his number, and I'd never felt so liberated. I switched to social media, and Brady's messenger box was lit up green.

. . .

Brady: *Long time no hear*

Ash: *Sorry, it's been manic*

Brady: *No worries. Wanna hear a funny story?*

Ash: *Always*

Brady: *Lucas ate an entire chocolate cake.*

Ash: *Shit.*

Brady: *Yep, lots of that. Plus puke. Everywhere. Word of advice, lock up all cake.*

Ash: *I'm on it*

Brady: *Good call*

Ash: *I have that meetup today. Are you sure you can't make it?*

Brady: ...

Brady: ...

Brady: *I wish I could, but I can't. I'm sorry to let you down.*

Ash: *You didn't let me down*

Brady: *I have to go, ttyl*

Ash: *Bye*

I packed for the expedition that was heading out to Nick's place, for the forum get-together. As I walked out, I saw Sean walking from his car, yawning.

He spotted me and headed straight over, swooping me into a kiss and then taking Mia from her seat and twirling her around.

Looping and bobbing in a big circle and with such a huge grin on his face that I fell for him that little bit more. They say the way to a man's heart is through his stomach, but for me it was clearly through loving Mia.

"We're going out," I explained when he looked down at the masses of stuff I had around me: bags, a box of tiny baby clothes to donate to the group, books for what they called a sanity exchange, along with a huge vanilla-frosted chocolate cake that was my food donation.

"Are you sure you're not *moving* out?" he quipped and then placed Mia into her seat and fastened her in, checking she was secure. She kicked her legs and waved her chubby hands, and he kissed her on the head again.

Jeez, what this man is doing to my heart.

"There's a lot to think of when you have a baby," I said.

He pulled me close and kissed me. Right in the front yard, in full view of everyone, and I didn't care at all. I wanted all the kisses and would hoard the feelings they created in me.

Hot, complicated feelings that were less about sex in general and more specifically about Sean.

"This is my first meeting of the Single Dads Together group."

He cradled my face. "Do you want me to go with the both of you? I could grab a shower."

I quirked a smile. "No offense, but you look like you need about eighteen hours sleep. Believe me, I know what I'm talking about. Also this is a single dads' group, not a single-dad-plus-hot-doctor-I'm-sleeping-with club." He winced a little, and I knew I'd fucked up with my throwaway joke. So I kissed away the frown. "I'll see you when I get back."

We kissed one final time, and then he hugged me. "Drive safe. Have fun."

Nick lived in a double-fronted house, in a gated community full of other huge houses, all with high-end cars in their driveway. This was exclusive with a capital E, and my car might have been new, but the Hyundai was out of place with the proliferation of Porsches, interspersed with the odd Maserati.

I whistled under my breath. "Jeez, Mia, what does this dude do for work?" I pulled the car onto the drive and killed the engine. Mia waved her fists at me and then examined her right hand as if it was the first time she'd seen it.

"I don't know anything about him or any of them," I said and smoothed a finger over her hair. My other hand tightened on the steering wheel, and my knuckles whitened. Mia was in her prettiest little outfit, the tiniest pair of dungarees I'd ever seen and a pink top, courtesy of Siobhan. I'd assumed babies wore sleepers until they were old enough to walk, but what do I know?

There was baby makeup out there apparently.

Makeup.

For babies.

Yeah, not happening. I'd packed and repacked my bag, taking exactly what I thought I'd need in the hope it didn't look as if I was moving house, and it appeared to most that I was a master of the mess that babies created.

When Sean had asked if I needed him, even coming

off two shifts and a training day, I'd almost said yes, but that wasn't the point of today. This was a single dads thing, and despite thinking all kinds of warm affectionate thoughts about Sean, he wasn't my partner, and he wasn't Mia's dad.

"I'll be fine," I muttered and got out of the car, opening the back door and unfastening the car seat. Mia's eyes were wide open, and I pulled down the brim of her pink hat to shade her eyes, then hefted the bag, cake, and the car seat to the large oak front door. After ringing the bell, I waited for the moment that people began to see through me, to the shaky nervous mess beneath.

A tall man opened the door, dark hair shot with gray at the temples. He had a wide smile and threw back the door with enthusiasm.

"You must be Ash. Come in. Come in."

I stepped inside the huge place, ending up in a hallway that could have been a room in its own right, a wide staircase curving around it and an honest-to-God galleried walkway lined with books on the floor above.

He held out a hand, then dropped it with a rueful shake of his head when he saw I had no free hand before relieving me of the cake box. "It was a year before I could ever shake hands again," he said. "I'm Nick. Come through. The rest are already here." I followed him through wide double doors and into a sitting room packed full of chairs, sofas, changing bags, babies, colorful toys, and in the middle of it, sitting on the floor, were a circle of men. They all looked up as I stepped in, and one of them stood and took my diaper bag off me.

"Gray," he said, and I was quickly introduced in turn to Austin, David, and Michael, who along with the host Nick, made up this branch of what Nick called the Single Dads Together San Diego support group.

Gray patted a space on the floor next to him, and I realized babies had the pride of place on the sofas, and I counted three that weren't much older than Mia. Three in identical sleepers or at least identical in all but the fact that they had different names on their chests; three babies who had to be related.

"Mine," Austin said with a smile. "Anna, Amy, and Aden, keeping with the A's. My surrogate had triplets."

All the energy left me suddenly, and I joined the others on the floor, the car seat next to me.

"You're joking."

Austin shook his head. I could tell he was exhausted, but he was also smiling. "Not at all, but I'm lucky I have a nanny, or a manny if you want to be precise. So I do get to share the work. My manny, Paul, is here, but he's in charge of coffee."

So Austin had triplets. Gray's boy was six. David and Michael sat so close to each other I swear there was something there, and between them, they had four children: three girls and a boy, all over ten. Then there was Nick, with his three, all of whom were in the house somewhere. Or so he explained.

Then it was my turn, and as I ate cookies and drank delicious dark coffee brought in by a very young-looking Paul-the-Manny, whose smile lighted the room, I explained about me.

"Darius, my ex, was with me when we initiated the

process, but I know that it was me wanting a family that split us up in the end. He left as soon as it properly began, told me it wasn't his life path. I could have stopped with the journey, no harm no foul. Only I wanted a child so badly that I carried on." I caught Austin's expression filled with compassion, and I knew he understood.

"Do you have a support network?" Gray asked, "A new partner? Family?"

"My sister is completely supportive, and until recently I was estranged from my mom, but she's back in my life, although things are still not entirely one hundred percent there."

"Were you estranged from your mom because you chose to have children?" David asked.

"That's what happened to me," Michael muttered.

"Their loss," David patted Michael's knee.

Then it was my turn to answer. The guys would understand. I knew they all had significant others who were men. "Mostly the fact that I'm gay."

"Preach," Austin muttered.

We exchanged smiles, and there was that understanding again. I felt like maybe I wasn't the only one to be going through all of this.

"I do feel…" I paused and thought about the word I needed to use to explain the enormity of everything.

"Alone?"

"Sad?"

"Angry at your ex?"

"Lonely?"

"Overwhelmed?"

Everyone spoke at once, but I could make out the individual things. "I'm not angry with Darius. I must admit I had this fantasy that one day he'd turn up and he'd see me with Mia and utterly regret leaving me. But now, I don't ever want him to see Mia, and when he asked me to go to New York to meet him on my own, I said no. He isn't ready to be a dad. I'm not sure he ever will be. But yeah, I do feel lonely." That was such a monumental thing to admit to a room full of men, but not one of them criticized me for feeling that way.

We talked for hours, and by the time I left, I had a phone full of email addresses, social media links, and cell numbers.

Nick extended a hand. "You know where we are."

I shook his hand and wanted to do something over the top like hug him until he squeaked, but I didn't. I was restrained and kept my emotions in check.

That was, until I stopped at the first red light and emotion stole my breath. So much, that I pulled over into a diner's parking lot until I calmed down.

How did it go? The text showed up from Sean while I was sitting there, and came with an added heart emoji. Talk about completely perfect timing.

Good. I sent back. *On my way home.*

I knew he was at home and that I could take Mia and go find him, just to spend time with him. I was certain Sean and I could be good together.

And I wanted that.

But how did I know when it was okay to allow someone into my life? We'd talked about that in the meeting. David and Michael had met through the group.

Nick had been single since his husband died. Austin and Gray both said they weren't even searching for anyone.

I hadn't exactly been looking. I'd had this entire life plan that I was going to follow: surrogacy, baby, happy life. Nowhere in there were any plans to fall for the hot doctor next door.

When we arrived home, Sean was waiting for us, sitting on our porch, coffee in hand, swinging gently on the old wooden swing. I wanted to blurt out that I liked him. That he scared me. That he made me feel warm and hopeful and turned on, and everything else in a confusing kaleidoscope of emotions.

He was perfect there on the seat, and when he moved to help us, there was a big part of me that wanted to tell him to go and sit back down.

I wanted to say that I would go and get my own coffee, and maybe we could both sit and rock, with Mia in my arms, or his, and watch the world go by.

But wasn't that too much like more than only being lovers or friends?

Wasn't that something a lot more dangerous?

NINETEEN

Sean

Somehow, I ended up sitting between Eric and Leo, when what I really wanted to do was sit with Ash. Only, Ash and Mia were in demand. Right now, they were surrounded by some of our other neighbors, and Mia was the center of attention at the end of season barbecue.

Ash and I had been a thing now for three months, actually twelve weeks and two days from that fateful night when Eric had knocked on his door.

Most of what we did as a couple was at his place. Sex. Kissing. Reading together. Watching films. Talking. It was all where we could watch Mia, and Ash and her owned my heart completely.

Was twelve weeks too soon to use the L-word?

"I'll be at Ringwood for the weekend of the fifteenth," Eric announced, peering at his phone and frowning. "It's the first weekend I have off."

I pulled out my cell and checked dates. "I can do Friday and all day Saturday until ten. Leo?"

Leo attempted to check his phone one-handed but had to let go of the tug toy with Cap trotting off proudly, having won that battle. I couldn't fail to notice that Cap sat next to Ash, leaned on his leg and stared up at him adoringly. I bet that is what I was like whenever we were together. All kinds of puppy dog needy. I snorted at the thought, and Eric sent me a sharp glance.

"What?"

"Nothing," I said and settled in the comfy chair, tilting my head back and waiting for Leo to check out available dates.

"I can do Saturday and into Sunday, until two."

"It's agreed then. The home sent a list through. They need bunkbeds, and two tiles are loose on the roof. Also, we have the garden to fix."

I nodded. The three of us having days off together was a miracle of management, but to have a weekend covered where all of us managed at least some of it was how we fitted in volunteering at Ringwood. I glanced stealthily at Ash and saw him staring back at me.

"What's Ringwood?" he asked, and I let Eric answer. He was the one who'd set it all up and was the de facto boss of the three of us when we began new projects.

"It's a foster home out on Murphy Canyon Road," he said. "We volunteer there sometimes, do some jobs, fix things up, gardening, that kind of thing."

"I like gardening," Ash said and then dipped his head. He was embarrassed, and I couldn't understand why. Then it hit me. He was volunteering in his own way, and was worried that we'd close ranks and say we didn't need anyone else. Or was that my own guilt talking? It had always been just the three of us, and it was something that I jealously guarded.

"We can always use the help," Leo said and then looked at me in a very deliberate way, as if he was waiting for me to herd the three of us together to the exclusion of anyone else.

"You could bring Mia," I said instead, and Eric snorted a laugh behind his hand. He mumbled something under his breath that sounded a lot like "you've got it bad, buddy."

But I didn't hear it clearly enough to call him on it. Instead, I thumped him on the arm, and he began to laugh so hard he fell out of his chair.

"Asshole," I muttered and stood up. "I want to show Mia the pool, can I?"

That set off a whole new round of laughing, but I ignored him, and with Ash and Mia in tow, we made our way down the garden and to the sparkling pool beyond. Several of the neighborhood kids were in there, splashing and playing around, and there was no way that Mia's first go in a pool was going to happen in this much chaos when it was this late. But that didn't stop Ash and me from sitting in the gathering dark in the pool chairs and chilling. I'd brought down two sodas from the cooler, and he took one gratefully.

"Do you enjoy volunteering?" he asked me as Mia batted at something and pursed her Cupid bow lips.

"Yeah, I do. Leo was in a foster home until the Byrnes found and adopted him. It's just a way of giving back."

"On top of working all hours keeping people alive?"

I side-eyed him, and he was smirking, the ass. What was it with people teasing me today?

"Whatever. I can't help being perfect." I could laugh at myself, and with Ash, it was all so natural.

"You're way too unflawed. In fact, you're dangerous."

This time he wasn't teasing; he was dead serious, and I turned in my chair. "Ash?"

"You think maybe we should say something about what we've been doing?" he asked and tucked a blanket over Mia's toes as if he needed something else to concentrate on. She kicked it off instantly; that was Mia, already stubborn and focused on what she did and didn't want. She was nearly five months now, and everything about her was perfect. In fact, everything about me and Ash was pretty perfect as well.

"What do you want to talk about?"

Ash cleared his throat. "When I'm with someone, I'm *with* them."

I nodded, not quite following what he meant, and then it hit me. "No other guys, you mean."

He sat upright, rigid. "I know you've had a lot of relationships, but that's a deal breaker."

I reached over and clasped his hand. "It's a deal breaker for me too."

He was confused for a moment and couldn't meet my gaze. "Eric said, that night he was drunk... He implied that I was one of your many hookups."

"Oh," I said and realized I was treading on dangerous ground here. "There've been guys you know, before you, one-night stands, few and far between though, and nothing like a relationship, and I was always safe and regularly tested. Yeah?" I held up a hand as he watched me. "We're having fun here, and I like it."

He frowned and then leaned forward, focused. "What if I want something different?"

"What do you mean?"

"Never mind, I don't know what I mean."

He couldn't mean an open relationship, given his first rule, but maybe I was being too intense? Maybe I should back off and calm the fuck down, even if I wanted to tell him I loved him and could he love me back?

Love. How had I fallen deeply in love with him so fast?

We sat quietly for a while, but by then, Mia needed her night bottle, and she had a routine that Ash didn't mess with. Because of that, she slept from ten until six, and I could tell the difference in Ash's face. He wasn't as exhausted as he used to be. In fact, he was in his element, and he'd hired a local woman to sit with Mia each morning so he could work. Then the rest of the day was his and Mia's, and he loved her so much it made my heart ache to see them together.

"I think we're going to head home."

I fought the disappointment that they were going, but hid it well, or at least I thought I did. After all, I could go over a little later, once Mia was asleep, and make love to Ash in the spare room. He'd decorated in there, subtle gold and red, with new rugs and bedding, and it was our temporary love nest. Mia was due to go into her own room, the nursery decorated in bright primary colors, and that meant the red room, as I'd started to call it, would be defunct.

I couldn't wait to make love to my man in his big bed with the wooden poles. So much to hang on to.

"You coming with me?" he asked after a pause.

"Yeah?"

He held out a hand, and I took it, and together we headed out. There were quite a few people still there, sprawled on the grass or sitting with their feet in the pool, and they all said good-bye, and no one batted an eyelid over the fact that the two guys holding hands were leaving. Leo winked at me, but then, I expected that and gave him the finger.

We made it all the way to his front door, and expectation burned in my chest. Not for sex or making love, but for the domestic chores of two people sharing care for a baby. He even had his key in the lock. We'd almost made it in.

"Ash," someone called from behind us, and I didn't have to be an expert in body language to understand that Ash was startled. He went rigid and turned on his heel to face the owner of the voice.

"Darius."

This was Darius? The ex who cheated on Ash? The one who'd backed away from the surrogacy at the last possible moment? Trepidation coiled inside me, and I knew I needed to stay calm if I could because Ash might need me.

"Hey, Ash." Darius' tone was light, and he smiled with what I assumed he thought was fondness. To me, it looked like a mix between a smirk and panic. "Is that the baby?" he asked, and I couldn't fail to see how protective Ash was as he tucked Mia in his arms.

"I've got nothing to say to you," Ash explained. He sounded as if he was over all of Darius' shit, but Darius wasn't getting the message.

Darius chuckled and made a tutting sound of disapproval.

What the hell?

"You don't mean that, sweetheart," Darius cajoled.

"I do."

"Can I see her?" Darius moved closer, and I stepped between Ash and Darius, a walking, talking roadblock.

"Why the he—why are you here?" Ash snapped, with none of the politeness I associated with the man I knew I loved.

"I'm here to talk, to apologize, to see you and talk about the next steps with the baby."

"What?" Ash sounded horrified, and my stomach was in knots.

"I'll get Leo," I said. "And Eric." Between the three of us, we could get Darius off of the porch.

"We don't need Leo, he's a cop and it could escalate," Ash said, and I watched Darius' nonchalant expression slip a little.

"Look, I just want to apologize."

"I don't need an apology. Now leave."

"Oh, Ash, come on, babe. Don't be like that," Darius coaxed. "Why don't we get someone to look after the baby, and we can talk."

"Mia, her name is Mia."

Darius frowned. "I don't recall that being on our list of names."

"*Your* list of names," Ash muttered.

"Let your friend take the—Mia—and we can talk." He then climbed the three steps and extended a hand to me. "I'm Darius, but I'm sure that you've heard of me."

I shook his hand, but not for long. Ash's ex-partner was a douche, and he acted as if he had a *right* to see Mia. Not to mention I'd just had the whole goddamned love epiphany in my head, and I needed to blurt out how I felt right here and now.

Darius released my hand and took a step around me to look at Ash, but Ash didn't move toward him, and I waited for a clue as to what he wanted me to do. I stood next to him in a united front.

"What do you want?" Ash asked again. There was a tone to his voice I'd never heard before: resignation.

"I said, we need to talk."

"No," Ash said, blunt and to the point.

"I just want to meet Mia and see if maybe we could try again. The three of us."

What the fuck? No.

Ash turned to hand Mia to me. There was a universe of trust in his eyes. I took her and cradled her close.

Then he cracked his neck. "Darius, when you were with me, you slept with three other men. At least three that I know of. You walked out on me and the plans we'd made, and I have a new life now."

Darius held out a hand. "But I want to apologize."

Was that going to be enough to convince Ash? I shuffled closer to him, and my elbow knocked his. I didn't know if it would help, but if he felt me there, maybe he could stay calm.

"No." Ash was emphatic. "I have nothing to say to you."

"We could be the family *you* wanted."

Ash narrowed his eyes. "What?"

Darius shrugged. "I have a new position in Scotland, or at least I will when the funding is agreed upon. There's a place there, a big house for a family."

"A family?" Ash asked, and my heart sank. Was he going to be swayed away from me and this small house in San Diego for a man in another country?

"Special houses just for families, with no cost. The new company likes families in the remote community, and I told them about you and the baby. Mia, I mean."

"And?"

"And that we were a family." He couldn't meet Ash's gaze and abruptly it all made sense to me and to Ash it seemed.

"What you mean is that the funding prerequisite from this new institution is that you have a family, and you told them you had one."

"Not exactly…" Even I could tell he was lying. Darius blustered a bit, even looked affronted that Ash could even suggest that. "But I may have implied—"

Ash touched Mia and bumped my arm. "This is my family," he interrupted.

My heart swelled, and I felt as if I had everything in that moment.

Darius wasn't letting it go. "Ash. Come on—"

"Goodbye, Darius."

Ash opened his front door and gestured for me to go in first. When we were inside, he shut and locked it behind us. "Shit," he muttered. "Sorry."

I shook my head. "Nothing to be sorry about."

He took Mia from me, and I reached for him, my heart full of love and the need to touch him, but he sidestepped me.

"You might want to wait to make sure he's gone before you leave. He's an idiot, and I wouldn't put it past him to be sitting out there, waiting to talk to me. He never did know how to listen." Ash began to walk upstairs, and I followed him.

"I'm not going yet. I want to help with Mia, kiss you, hug you a bit." *Maybe talk about how I'm in love with you and Mia.*

He rounded on me at the top of the stairs. "We were having fun, but somewhere along the way, I made the mistake of falling in love with you." He made it sound as if it was a bad thing, and I waited for the *but.*

I needed to defend what happened. "That's not a mistake—"

"It's okay though. I have Mia to think about, and now you have to leave before I promise myself everything will always be okay. When I do stupid things like that, I ignore all the red flags of when things fall apart."

He went into the master bedroom, and I was too confused to follow at first, and then I unpicked what he'd just said.

"Whoa," I said and stalked after him, Mia was on the changing mat, and he was cleaning her and getting her ready for bed, and I had a *lot* to say. "Now, wait a minute. I fell in love with you too," I blurted, which wasn't exactly how I thought I'd be telling him. He finished closing the snaps on Mia's tiny sleeper and lifted her off the mat.

"Mia needs her bottle."

I let him move past me, and then at the last minute, I scooted around him and blocked his exit. How did I make him see that I wasn't messing with him? Or that he did have space in his heart for me as well as Mia?

Mia. That was my inspiration.

"I will personally vet the first boy that dates Mia. Or I'll get her uncle Leo to arrest him and question him first."

He blinked at me. "What?"

"I'll make sure that the first day of school I'll hold one hand when you hold the other, and when they ask who her daddies are, I hope to hell that she says you and me. We'll take her swimming, and when you're working, maybe I can be the one who plays with her or takes her shopping. I'll help her with homework, and I'll be there when she rides her first bike. I love you, Ash, and I want forever with you."

His eyes widened. "I can't do this. It's not just me I have to think about."

"I know you're scared—"

"You don't know anything about how terrified I am, Sean. When I found out that Darius had slept with other guys, had unprotected sex, put my life in danger, I rationalized it. But I could come to terms with the infidelity because I was okay. I made it out the other side intact. But I have Mia now, and she is my priority."

"I wouldn't hurt her or you."

"I know."

"Then why won't you let me in?"

Ash laid Mia on his quilt, protected her from rolling off with strategic cushions. Then he turned to me and crossed his arms over his chest, defensively. "Because I'm scared, okay? And it's completely rational for me to feel that way, so don't you dare tell me that I shouldn't be scared."

He was scared? I was terrified. What if this was it? What if he was pushing me out of his life and Mia's?

"I wouldn't—"

"I can't have an affair right now."

An affair? Is that what he thought we had going here? Did he not understand that I loved him completely?

"When we were on the porch, you handed me Mia," I said and waited for him to process that. "You gave me the most precious thing in your life, and you knew I'd take care of her. Right?"

After a short pause, he nodded, and I let him think on his actions and for him to realize that he trusted me, heart and soul, and that I had no intention of hurting him or Mia.

"I love you, Ash. And I love Mia. We could be a family."

His legs gave way under him, and he sat on the mattress next to Mia, holding out his hand for her to grip his thumb.

"I don't have room in my heart—"

"Yes, you do. Even if it's a tiny space right there next to Mia and your family, I'll make sure I fit."

"Sean…"

"I won't be taking anything away from you and Mia. I promise you that I will add to your lives, and I will always be there for you." God, now I was sounding desperate. If Ash didn't want me around, then trying to persuade him otherwise would be stupid. I couldn't force him to want me. "Please just… I love both of you." There, I'd said everything I was going to say, and now the ball was in Ash's court. "I'll be next door."

"What do you think, Mia?" he asked, and I stopped right at the door to the bedroom and waited. "Do you think we can do this? Let Sean in? Would you like to try having two daddies instead of one?"

I heard Mia gurgle, and I turned to face them.

A cautious smile curved Ash's lips. "We love you, too." The relief was incredible, and I sat on the opposite side of him and took her hand in mine. She gripped my shirt and held on tight. I took Ash's hand, and the three of us hugged.

It was the perfect family circle.

Brady: *Is it always this hard?*

Ash: *Are you okay?*

Brady: *Bad day. Maddie hates me. Lucas wants to stab me with a fork.*

. . .

I reread that last part and wondered if maybe that was another word that had been modified by spell check.

Ash: *A fork?*

Brady: *Yeah. Tell me something to cheer me up. I'm done with today.*

Ash: *I have really good news. Sean said he loved me, and I admitted I loved him. We're in love.*

Brady: *Wow.*

Ash: *I know!*

Brady: *I'm so pleased for you both. I can't wait to meet him.*

Ash: *You should come over. You're not far.*

There was a big pause and not even any dancing dots.

Ash: *You still there?*

Brady: *Sorry, yes. I have to go, but congratulations, Ash.*

Ash: *Is everything okay?*

Brady: *Is anything ever okay? Sorry, ignore me. Talk later.*

He signed off with a smiley face, thumbs-up, champagne bottles, two men together, and a baby. I think he was overcompensating.

I sent back a heart and logged off.

"You okay in here?" Sean asked from the door. He had Mia in his arms.

"I'm just coming."

I'll talk to Brady tomorrow. See if I can't help. Maybe one day he'd let me.

Epilogue

ASHER

One Year Later

The annual barbecue was different from last year. Instead of swimming trunks, I wore a suit. Instead of soda, there was champagne. And Mia was no longer a tiny helpless baby; she was sixteen months old and walking confidently between the people sitting on the chairs. She stopped at her uncle Leo, who scooped her up and held her close to him. He was chief Mia wrangler, or at least he was half of the wrangling team; Eric was the other half and was around here somewhere.

"Hello, sweetheart."

"Hi, guys."

I hugged Siobhan and her husband, Dan, who was back from his final tour and had taken to life Stateside as an Army instructor like a duck to water.

I hugged Mom and she had tears in her eyes, although I really think they were tears of joy. We had tried our hardest this year to find middle ground; back to a place where we could love each other. Even if it may never be an unconditional love we were getting closer and I was at least beginning to trust her. Having Sean and Mia in my life made this easy. Between them, they filled my life with pure love. Because of this I had some over I could try to give to my mom, and mostly it was working.

"Don't cry," I told my mom as we hugged. She dabbed at her eyes after, and smiled at me.

"I'm just so happy."

"Me too."

Brady waved at me from a couple of rows back, a slim, dark-haired guy in a charcoal suit. Finally I was going to meet my messenger friend, face-to-face, rather than through the messages we exchanged. He was still an enigma to me, one day up, the next day down, and it had taken everything in me to get him to come here today. He'd brought Lucas and Maddie with him, although he said it had been hard to get them to come.

I could tell from here that Lucas was on his phone, and Maddie had her arms folded over her chest with a mutinous expression marring her pretty face. I waved back, and he smiled at me, although he immediately shrunk in his chair. I couldn't wait to talk to him, find out more about him, give him a hug that he can carry home to help him when he was down. We talked nearly every evening about one thing or another, but sometimes I think he just needed that hug. I'd seated him with my family because he was my first real non-Darius friend.

Eric moved past me, and I caught his arm. "Can I ask you a favor?"

"Sure thing." Eric smiled at me and waited patiently.

"Third row, dark-haired guy with two children. Can you keep an eye out for him?"

Eric looked where I was gesturing, and smiled. "Easily."

"We have to sit," Mom interrupted and went to take a seat. Pride emanated from her as she took her turn holding Mia, getting a face full of sticky kisses in the process. Dan sat next to her and handed his mother-in-law a wipe. This was simple domestic stuff that made me smile.

"You doing okay, little brother?" Siobhan asked and straightened my tie. I swear it was straight, but I think Siobhan just needed something to do with her hands.

I caught one of them and held tight. "I'm more than okay," I said.

She embraced me. "I love you," she murmured.

The tone of the music changed, less soft love songs and more processional.

"That's my cue," I said, and she pressed a kiss on the tip of my nose before wiping at it with her hand.

"Oops, sorry. I don't imagine a scarlet-tipped nose will show up in photos."

"Siobhan—"

"I'm kidding. Now go do this thing."

She left then to collect Mia, and I sauntered to my place. Sean was already there, standing straight, in a pale gray suit, white shirt, and sapphire tie. His eyes were stunning. He was gorgeous. I loved him, and he was mine.

And today we were getting married.

Eric and Leo joined us, along with Siobhan, who carried Mia. I took Mia from her, and Sean held Mia's hand.

It was a simple ceremony, perfect.

"I love you and Mia. You are the better parts of me," Sean murmured his vows so that some of them only I could hear.

My vows were short and sweet. "I love you, Sean. I will always love you."

The last word though was for Mia.

She touched my cheek. Then she leaned into my hold so she could pat Sean's face before giving us wet kisses.

"Daddas," she exclaimed, and my heart melted. I held my family tight and said a silent thank you for this perfect life, filled with love, hope, and plans for the future.

How lucky can one single dad get?

THE END

What's next in single Dads?

Single

Today

Promise

Always

Today, Single Dads book 2

When the world labels a man and judges them blindly, is it possible to ever find love?

Firefighter Eric is on the front line, battling the threat of nature's destruction in the California grasslands alongside his CalFire team. Focused and calm, even in the direst of situations, he has a strong affection for his fire truck, loves his career, and has best friends he can rely on. All he needs now is love, but that seems to be impossible to find. At his friend's wedding, Eric falls in lust at first sight with the shy, slim and sexy Brady, even if Brady isn't the type of guy he usually goes for. What Eric longs for is an equal in his bed, not a smaller guy who might want Eric to role-play big strong firefighter every time they have sex. He wants to find someone he can be vulnerable with, someone who will love him for his soft heart and quiet ways.

Brady's life plans grind to a halt when his niece and nephew lose their parents in a tragic accident, and he becomes a dad overnight. His Developmental Coordination Disorder rules his life, but he fights both DCD and the fears that chase him every day, to give Maddie and Lucas a home. Agreeing to go to a friend's wedding is a decision he regrets long before he even gets there. But, he refuses to give in to his fear, even if he might do something that makes him a target for people's comments and laughter. Meeting Eric, a huge man with a gentle voice and a flair for chivalry, he falls hard. Now, if only he can let himself get past his panic that Eric would never want someone like him, then maybe he could fall in love for real.

Newsletter

To keep up to date with news and releases I have a monthly newsletter alongside tailored bulletins for different sales outlets whenever there is a new release, or I make a book free, or have a sale.

You can select which newsletter groups you want to sign up for and it all starts here:

rjscott.co.uk

Meet RJ Scott

RJ is the author of the over one hundred published novels and discovered romance in books at a very young age. She realized that if there wasn't romance on the page, she could create it in her head, and is a lifelong writer.

She lives and works out of her home in the beautiful English countryside, spends her spare time reading, watching films, and enjoying time with her family.

The last time she had a week's break from writing she didn't like it one little bit and has yet to meet a bottle of wine she couldn't defeat.

www.rjscott.co.uk | rj@rjscott.co.uk

NEWSLETTER

- facebook.com/author.rjscott
- twitter.com/Rjscott_author
- instagram.com/rjscott_author
- bookbub.com/authors/rj-scott
- pinterest.com/RJ_LoveLane

Printed in Great Britain
by Amazon